How To Save The U.S.A.

Harry D. Reynolds

iUniverse, Inc.
New York   Bloomington

iUniverse books may be ordered through booksellers or by contacting:

iUniverse
1663 Liberty Drive
Bloomington, IN 47403
www.iuniverse.com
1-800-Authors (1-800-288-4677)

Because of the dynamic nature of the Internet, any Web addresses or links
contained in this book may have changed since publication and may no longer be
valid. The views expressed in this work are solely those of the author and do not
necessarily reflect the views of the publisher, and the publisher hereby disclaims
any responsibility for them.

ISBN: 978-1-4401-6966-3 (sc)
ISBN: 978-1-4401-6967-0 (ebook)

Printed in the United States of America

iUniverse rev. date: 10/07/2009

Table of Contents

Author's Notes

The Chapter's titles and topics are in no particular order, they are just in the order that my thoughts came to me. I am not naive, I realize that the solutions that I have proposed are SIMPLE, for very complex problems. Before you become an elitist and claim that I have given childish answers to adult questions, you might want to consider the following: Albert Einstein's equation for the theory of relativity is beautiful, because it is SIMPLE. Paintings and photographs can be very beautiful, with SIMPLE subjects. Music can be beautiful, with SIMPLE melodies or topics, example White Christmas. Abraham Lincoln's Gettysburg Address is beautiful in its SIMPLICITY. Martin Luther King's, I have a dream speech is beautiful. One of the reasons is the SIMPLE statement, "You will in the future not be judged by the color of your skin, but by the content of your character." We need to start this method of judgment now and end all references to the color of your skin. John F. Kennedy's speech which included the statement "Ask not what your country can do for you, but what you can do for your country?" is also beautiful, because it is SIMPLE. That question, "What can you do for your country?" can now be answered. The people must take their rightful place as the leaders of this country. You can do this by being informed. You can then vote for the people who have the answers, not just vote party affiliation. The next step is to keep in touch with your representatives on a regular basis.

The AUW contract with the Auto companies is around 4,000 pages, it is not beautiful, because it is COMPLICATED. This contract should be scrapped, see the chapter on unions. The United States Income Tax Code is somewhat short of one million pages and growing. It is not beautiful, because it is COMPLICATED. This also needs to be scrapped, see my chapter on the Federal Income Tax System. The United States Senate in the years 2007 and 2008 introduced 10,327 bills and resolutions. No one senator read one-tenth of these documents, let alone understood them. Yet they voted on them. If anyone can tell me, without looking it up, three problems they solved, then they should be writing this book. Beyond complicated it is downright unbelievable.

I have found in my life that the best solutions to problems are not COMPLICATED, they are SIMPLE. I have put a blank page after each chapter for you to make notes, this will make it easier to become involved.

Finally to quote Albert Einstein: "Out of clutter find simplicity, from discord find harmony, in the middle of difficulty lies opportunity." This sums up our present state of affairs, cluttered to say the least, with discord and all kinds of difficulties. The result is that opportunities abound to solve these problems with simple solutions.

Sincerely,

Harry D. Reynolds

First Saturday Of Each Month

Chapters in My Life:

Harry the Retiree

Harry the Father, Grandfather, and Great Grandfather

Harry the Realtor

Harry the Small Business Owner, Farmer

Harry the Mechanical Engineer

Harry the Student

Harry the Soldier and Military Draftee

Harry the Midwesterner

Harry the Rebel

Preface

What can be right with America?

Picture: The living room of all the homes in the USA. This book is laying on the floor all dog eared, with notes written on every page.

The Caption reads:
"We are going to make a difference."

Is there anybody out there who cares? Great! Lets get started on fixing this great country of ours. Read the book, then pick a problem or problems and start solving them. Why not get all your friends and acquaintances to help. If you think you might care or you just don't know what to do about how you feel, read the book. There is a problem for everyone to get excited about. You can make a difference, we just have to make a difference or the problems will overwhelm the country. We are getting close to that point, so the country needs your help now. If you don't care period, why have you picked up this book? I dare you to read it and you will become enlightened, or if nothing else it will become a conversational starter if left on your coffee table. I let a friend of mine read an early draft. Yes, he is liberal and he became only interested in how I earned my money. He told me he did skip over parts and his only comment about it was that we think differently. Being an optimist I cannot believe that people don't care. What have you got to lose from caring? Oh yes, he did say the problem with education was not enough money. Wow! If money could solve problems, the United States would have no problems. George Soros read the book your name is in it. Warren Buffet your name is there also. One question for you: Since you are a good Democrat, would you mind telling me what taxes you paid last year? I'm sure its a small percentage of your wealth compared to my percentage. By the way you made a big donation to the Gates Foundation. If the Gates foundation of the future becomes a clone of the Ford Foundation on steroids, please, buy all my books and burn them, because there will be no fixing America. America haters, put the book down and immigrate to Venezuela, yes, Michael Moore that means you. Congress, read the book and then get to work and do the right thing. Mr. President, use this book to build a legacy that will make you the most popular president ever, think statue in the Washington National Mall. People who are concerned about the environment, read the book and see how we can shape history. Environmental wackos put the book down and go protest at congress about all the flatulence.

Acknowledgements

I want to thank all who encouraged me to complete this project. Without your encouragement there would have been times it would have been easy to quit. Special thanks to Ted Rebello for his word cartoon ideas, which made me think of them also. It added a new dimension to the book. Thank you " iuniverse" for being patient with an amateur. Thank you, to all the people who read various early drafts, must have been awful. Your comments were graciously accepted, well, I would like to think so anyway. A very special thanks to Russell Kirk for allowing me include his "Ten Conservative Principles" in this book.

Introduction

I am going to assume that you are not reading this book for its literature value but for its innovative ideas and its passion. "I are an engineer not a literature scholar." I only considered writing this, my first book, because I became so incensed during the campaign leading up to the last election. I have tried to introduce simple ideas to make this a better country. The only way any of this can happen will be by the passion generated in the electorate. This passion will be created when we realize that the country is run by the voters. I hope you will enjoy the word cartoons and the messages that I tried to convey. Dig deep and find your own passion, so together, we can enjoy a better America.

Chapter One

What is wrong with America?

Picture: A person sitting in front of a television set, throwing a book at it. The newspapers, ripped apart, are scattered all over the floor. The radio in the background has been yelled at.

The Caption reads:
"The reason I am writing this book"

Life experiences that have culminated in writing this book

What motivated me to write this book? It was the 2008 Presidential election. Both candidates promised change but with very, very few specifics. We will probably just get more of the same, but with better articulation.

My first try to influence this election was to post this note to a blog. "Here is the solution to the problems we face: Elect whomever you want for President but congress is a different thing. I will keep this simple for the brain dead out there. Start a campaign to vote out every incumbent, this would send a message to Washington that would be heard around the world." The only problem was, blogs are all about expressing your opinion, nobody is listening.

We, as a country have the:

- "War on poverty"
- "War on drugs"
- Financial Crisis
- Immigration problem

- Global Warming Crisis, whatever that is? The last Ice age was 20,000 or so years ago, could be still warming.
- Not to forget the "War on Terror."
- The Health care crisis
- Social Security Problem almost a crisis
- Energy crisis
- Education, an on going problem
- Welfare problem

We must also mention the problem of using war as a solution to world problems. These are just the major problems facing this country. The previous administrations never made a dent in any of these, so the new President elect is going to solve these problems with the same old methods? I doubt it. I will take all odds on him not solving two of these problems, I would say one but they might get lucky. It is time for common sense to take over along with conservative ideas and get us out of this mess. We as citizens of this potentially super great country, must start taking an interest in what is happening. Get involved and make a difference. Read this book, pick your favorite problem and get involved to help solve it. You may have some different approaches to a problem, lets just solve them.

One of my first political memories would be my folks and all their friends gathered around the radio to listen to the results of the Roosevelt/Dewey election. All present were staunch Democrats. The only reason, I can think of now, that would make them stay democrats would be the promises that were being made to laborers. Little did I know that all the policies from the Roosevelt years would have such a continuing effect on life in America. Growing up I saw my dad, a union worker, get laid off on a continual basis each year, with union and government assistance, we survived. Looking back, I am sure this persuaded me to look for a better way. I think that without the war, which resulted in prosperity, Roosevelt's liberal ways would have gone by the wayside. This may be just what we have to watch for. If President Obama figures this out, we will be in war like situations in the future for all the same reasons, to promote an agenda. The next lesson I learned was that if I wanted something, I had to earn the money to buy it. Thanks Mom and Dad. I went to work in various professions, paper boy, shoveling snow, etc. Later I landed a real job. Looking back, I believe I was hired with no qualifications because there was no minimum wage and I was willing to work for 25 cents/hour. I soon learned the harder I worked the more I was appreciated and given raises. Within the first year I was up to $1/hour and I was becoming rich over night! During my high school career I worked several different types of jobs. I could not afford to go to college, or so I thought, so I volunteered for the draft and went into the Army for two years. This is where my education began. Gambling, loan sharking, but best of all I found out that there was a great big world out there and I could be whatever I wanted to be. When I was discharged from the army, I moved from Nebraska to California. By the way while I was in the army, I found that I could get promoted, with hard work. I started college in California and found jobs easily. What a lesson that was, when I applied for a job in California all had to say was, I had just moved from Nebraska and I was hired immediately. This was because of my expected work ethic, and they were never disappointed. I did not have the GI bill for schooling because of the particular years I was in the service. I applied for a loan for schooling and was always turned down, or offered such a small amount that it was not worth while. I told them to stuff their money, I could make it on my own. I learned that this was a typical government program: looks good on paper but the devil is in the details. During and after college I worked for the same company for 10 years, moving my way up through the ranks. At the end of those 10 years they showed me where I was vested in their pension plan and could retire in 31 more years, at a very good salary. I could not face the thought of another 31 years in the same place so I resigned and found another position immediately. It paid nearly twice my previous salary. I worked for them for one year then the bottom fell out of the economy and I was laid off. I started my own business and immediately went broke. I went down to the unemployment office to collect unemployment benefits. They told me I did not qualify because I had gone into business for myself, even though I had paid 10 years of unemployment taxes. I told them to stuff the money, I did not need anybody to take care of me, I would do it myself. I think then that I learned a very important truth, poverty is a mental disease, and it can be cured. I then went back to my business and made it happen. Eighteen years later I retired a millionaire, 13 years before my social security would start. Now social security covers one-fifth to one-sixth of my expenses. All government has to do is get out of the way.

I was in a business where I hired illegal aliens. I always paid them at least the minimum wage, some even earned two or three times that amount. The real story here is that I was unable to deduct their wages as an expense, without a social security number, so I would assign them one. When I made my quarterly reports their numbers were never questioned as long as their names were of Mexican lineage. Once I hired a new worker, an American citizen with a common name. When I submitted the quarterly report I assigned him a number instead of using his real number. Social security got back to me in days telling me it was the wrong number. I have always wondered how all the other money was absorbed into the system. My worst fear is that during that period, 35 to 40 years ago, what if an employer made a mistake on an American citizens social security number and his last name was Gonzales?

Another event in my life that effected my thinking was that I married a woman from England. Her father had a trucking business, when the labor government came into power in 1949, they nationalized his business. He was paid in government bonds maturing at par in 1983. Their face value over the intervening years varied in the 80% to 90% value. He was paid 3% interest but 1.5% was deducted in taxes as unearned income. Naturally in 1983 when they reached par they were worth a fraction of their value in 1949. This almost destroyed a good and hard working individual. How's that for a great liberal idea? We have to save America from this type of abuse because it appears to be heading this way, look out!

My brother took another path in life. He worked out of a teamsters union hiring hall. He knew exactly how many minutes he had to work to get the maximum unemployment benefits, for the maximum allowable time. He collected those benefits for at least 25 years. Great system huh? We have numerous lifetime welfare recipients out there because of this type of system. We must address these and other problems with this government. Our present generation seem to just want their work place to provide a retirement after 20 years or so. What happened to "pride in one's work?" The unions have pushed businesses like the auto industry into providing pensions starting at 55 years old. Great idea but they should be funded separately, not run like the governments social security program where the money is used for on going expenses. The number of pensioners just keeps increasing so the system cannot sustain itself. With life spans getting longer, retirements should be postponed unless the individual can fund it himself. This can easily be done with my government tax solution. Savings will not be taxed, this would include any interest on the savings that is not spent. I funded my own retirement plan, (this was a tax deferred plan) and retired at 50 years old. My social security plan will allow you to retire at the age of 65 with a very good income.

We must break the cycle of apathy and dependancy, because the next step is socialism, think third world country. Get out there and do something even if it's only giving money to organizations that are doing something. The saying, "If you are not part of the solution, you are part of the problem," is true. Just do it!

I have in this book tried to layout solutions to the various problems. Liberty and responsibility are inseparable, therefore I hope that the general public will get active and demand that the elected officials start solving these problems and not keep just making them worse. See Chapter 27, item 20 for our ultimate weapon to get their attention and keep their feet to the fire.

Notes

Fill in for future use

Name of your Representative_____

Address_____

E-mail Address_____

Phone Number_____

Name of your Senator_____

Address_____

E-mail Address_____

Phone Number_____

President Obama

Address_____

E-mail Address_____

Phone Number_____

Chapter Two

What is wrong with America?

Picture: A large person taking money from you and your employer, then, giving a small amount back to you when you are older.

The Caption reads:
"Why would we want the government in charge of our retirement?"

Social Security System

Our present social security system is going to fail and fail big, it cannot continue on it's present path. We need to fix it, a suggestion or two: Keep the present system in place for anyone over the age of 40. This will cost the government more money than we can count but it does have to stop sometime and it will be a permanent fix. It will be a government expenditure over 50 years, then the government will be free of this debt and will be able to reduce our taxes big time.

First thing that needs to be done is put everyone under the same system, there is no reason that certain government workers and other special interest groups have their own government retirement plans. Riddle me this why do the two paragraphs below look like a much better system than social security.

The Civil Service Retirement Act, which became effective on August 1, 1920, established a retirement system for certain Federal employees. It was replaced by the Federal Employees Retirement System (FERS) for Federal employees who first entered covered service on and after January 1, 1987.

The Civil Service Retirement System (CSRS) is a defined benefit, contributory retirement system. Employees share in the expense of the annuities to which they become entitled. CSRS covered employees contribute 7, 7 1/2 or 8 percent of pay to CSRS and, while they generally pay no Social Security retirement, survivor and disability (OASDI) tax, they must pay the Medicare tax (currently 1.45 percent of pay). The employing agency matches the employee's CSRS contributions.

Social Security payments by workers and employers should continue at the present number, except the top end should be raised to $3,000,000 or so. Yes, I understand that this is an unfair burden, but this failed system must be bailed out somehow. The money collected from the first $50,000, and one-half of the amount collected from $50,000 to $150,000 should be put into a fund for each individual. The balance of the money would be used to help the government pay the older individuals in the present system and others over 40 who will remain in the present system. Once the older individuals pass on, the top end should be reduced to $150,000 and all monies should be put into the individuals account. This mutual fund for lack of a better name should not be managed by money managers but be managed by a computer with a set formula. I would envision something like:

- 8% in the Dow tracking stock
- 10% in the S&P tracking stock
- 8% in the NASDAQ tracking stock
- 10% in the Russell 2000 indices
- 19% in tracking stocks of world markets, based upon the size of the various markets.
- 30% divide this in the various bond markets, AAA rated industry bonds and various city, state, and federal government bonds.
- 15% in various tracking stocks of currencies and commodities, including the United States dollar, oil and precious metals.

This portfolio should be rebalanced on a regular basis, this would smooth out all the bubbles. This money should only be accessed for retirement, or, in the case of death it would be part of the persons estate.

Individuals aged 40 (in the new system), based on a life expectancy of 90 years, who's earnings averaged $50,000 per year, would, at a conservative estimate, receive approximately $2,000/month upon retirement at 65. Individuals aged 30 (in the new system), based on a life expectancy of 100 years, who's earnings averaged $50,000 per year, would, at a conservative estimate, receive approximately $3,500/month upon retirement at 65. Computer models would be able to predict a more accurate estimate, using history as a guide. These numbers would be larger than any existing social security payouts. An added benefit is that your heirs do not lose this money, if you die before collecting it. Should you die at 66 years of age, the money paid to your heirs would approach $500,000. (This figure will vary with your lifetime earnings.)

At some point the government should get a small percentage of the monies contributed to insure an income for dependents of deceased workers. This is part of the existing social security system. This could be insured by a private company, I am sure it would be cheaper that way. In the present system social security contributions are used for many programs not related to retirement. These non related programs should be part of overall tax expenditures.

The following is a part of the Democratic 2008 Platform.

Retirement and Social Security

We will make it a priority to secure for hardworking families the part of the American Dream that includes a secure and healthy retirement. Individuals, employers, and government must all play a role. We will adopt measures to preserve and protect existing public and private pension plans. In the 21st century, Americans also need better ways to save for retirement. We will automatically enroll every worker in a workplace pension plan that can be carried from job to job and we will match savings for working families who need the help. We will make sure that CEOs can't dump workers' pensions with one hand while they line their own pockets with the other. At platform hearings, Americans made it clear they feel that's an outrage, and it's time we had leaders who treat it as an outrage. We will ensure all employees who have company pensions receive annual disclosures about their pension fund's investments, including full details about which projects have been invested in, the performance of those investments and appropriate details about probable future investments strategies. We also will reform corporate bankruptcy laws so that workers' retirements are a priority for funding and workers are not left with worthless IOU's after years of service. Finally, we will eliminate all federal income taxes for seniors making less than $50,000 per year. Lower- and middle-income seniors already have to worry about high health care and energy costs; they should not have to worry about tax burdens as well.

We reject the notion of the presumptive Republican nominee that Social Security is a disgrace; we believe that it is indispensable. We will fulfill our obligation to strengthen Social Security and to make sure that it provides guaranteed benefits Americans can count on, now and in future generations. We will not privatize it.

My Comments:

It is not a disgrace it is down right criminal, and lawmakers should admit it. They will not privatize it, the question is why? The answer is so that they can hold a big hammer over the head of the retiree's. You will notice that there is nothing but promises, that the government will be controlling every aspect of your retirement savings. Look at my solution, it will not self destruct in the future and it will pay the retiree a much better return on their social security withholdings. The government is using the social security withholding as a general tax on all people, and it is biased to make the lower income people pay a bigger percentage of their wages, in taxes. If you think your withholding is going into some sort of fund you have been brainwashed by the lawmakers. Right now an average worker, averaging $50,000/year, working 45 years will pay some where close to $300,000 in his lifetime and will collect about $480,000, if he lives to 85 years old. For all you math genius out there, what kind of return on your money after 65 years is that. If you earn an average of $82,000, you will have paid in about the same as you will get out. If you die early guess what, nearly all that money is donated to the government. Thanks! Another reason that they do not want to privatize your social security is that you now look to the government for your livelihood. Get them out of our lives, change the system now. It will not be privatized, it will be managed by the government as a thank you for paying taxes. They will collect the money and put it into the fund and pay your retirement from your fund.

One more try at explaining how the present social security system works. The government is using the social security withholding as a general tax on all people, and it is biased to make the lower income people pay a bigger percentage of their wages, in taxes. The government collects taxes from every one who works and all the workers employers. The employers portion of the taxes are your wages in disguise. Then when you reach their latest version of retirement age they pay you a monthly social security income, loosely based on the amount of social security taxes that you paid. I do mean loosely, it is their version of fair. I pointed out in my above comments that most people in the future will never even get back the amount of their contributions. Contributions, a good word, but not quite right, more like mandatory taxes disguised as contributions.

Notes on Social Security

Chapter Three

What is wrong with America?

Picture: A school building with graffiti all over it, with money being thrown at the building. The kids are hanging around outside, their teachers begging them to come inside to be educated.

The Caption reads:
"Who is in charge of educating the children?"

Education System

Education is the key to a life of prosperity, it has also been proven to extend your life expectancy. Education also gives you a better awareness of the world we live in, a better understanding of different cultures and a higher tolerance for work that can bring greater rewards later in life. Education is also the key to better government. We need an educated electorate to elect the people who will solve the problems of this great country. This electorate should keep the elected officials informed of their wishes. Generally the electorate should be the watch dogs of government.

The main problem with education is the national government. Right now it dictates strong guidelines to all States. As an example: Although the Constitution assigns the federal government no role in local education, Washington's authority over the nation's schools has increased dramatically. In less than a decade, annual federal funding has shot up 41 percent to almost $25 billion, while the regulatory burden on state and local governments has risen by about 6.7 million hours, and added $141 million in costs, during that time. The Federal Government should not be involved with the educational system, other than some simple basic rules. No where in the constitution does it give the national government any authority over education, therefore it should be the responsibility of each State. Education needs to be taken down to the local level, State regulated but locally run. This approach to education will create much competition resulting in excellent schooling. When competition happens, everyone will benefit. It will create better facilities, teachers, parent involvement and most important better grades and achievements by the students. We do not need professionally run unions involved with education. They only create huge bureaucracies. This large managerial staff is one of educations biggest problems. Teachers and educators should still be able to form committees to discuss working conditions and pay scales. If education is to be really effective, it must be possible to rid the work place of the ineffective teachers, with the present unions this has become impossible. Money is a major contributer to excellent results but it is being used in the complex management of the educational system. We need to get the money down to the teacher and student level. The unions hold back the really good and effective teachers. The really good teachers should be paid accordingly but the unions stop this by making a "one size fits all policy" based on seniority. One criticism of this will be, who determines who is a good teacher? It can only be determined by student results. The books being used in the system are selected by who knows who? Whilst parents cannot be allowed to select school books their ideas should be considered. Surely it should be possible for people to see a list of selected books and the reasons why they were chosen? Books must be selected for their learning content not bias (liberal, religion, etc.) of any kind. The school buildings and grounds are under used and way more elaborate than is required for teaching students how to think for themselves and learn the basics of knowledge. Parents should be able to choose which school their children attend. There should be flexibility rather than strict rules governing home location and school attended. Most of the educational dollar should go with the student so that private schools can be encouraged to compete with public schools for students. Home schooling should remain a choice, with controlled supervision.

Maybe one way to eliminate the unions from education would be to start all new schools then rehire teachers and administrative staff. This could be done on a gradual basis to avoid disruption to classes. Preferably it should be done during the summer holidays and be in place for the beginning of the school year.

The present method of accrediting and certifying teachers should be thoroughly reviewed. Other ways should be investigated to qualify teachers. Individuals from industry who are experts in their field should be able to give classes. Even parents and especially grandparents who have specialized fields should be able to teach, supervision and review would be necessary. Teachers should be paid by results not by seniority or longevity. Results should be based on student testing only. There should be no social or age promotions, only testing results should qualify a student for grade promotion. All schools should be accountable to the community and parents.

Discipline must be available to teachers. Parents must be responsible for sending a well disciplined child to school with some sort of penalties for parents of unruly children.

Teachers and school leaders should have the flexibility and authority to create successful learning environments.

The use of novel approaches to motivate the students and parents should be tried. Some possibilities are:

- Pay students to succeed. This is being tried in various locations, with good results and the money that is doing the motivating is mostly donated.

- Pay parents to attend night classes on how to help their child succeed in school.

- Regular lectures at school from outside businesses, community service organizations, heaven forbid, even religious organizations that have a positive message to give the students.

- Increase the number of work programs with outside businesses. There should be no minimum wage for this program. First year students in this program should be paid a minimum amount with merit raises to create incentive. This should be closely monitored.

- The school day should be extended to at least 8 hours per day, with breaks. Perhaps bring back a study hour or two with a monitor present to give advice on how to make the most of study time.

- Inter-school scholastic competition should be part of the schools program. There is nothing like competition to bring out the best in a child. Debates should be an integral part of schooling, current affairs would be a place to find excellent topics.

- Schools should have school uniforms, this would remove many social pressures and give students an identity. Most of the really successful schools have a uniform code and a disciplinary code of conduct. "The inmates must not be allowed to run the asylum."

For a much more in-depth coverage and insight into the problems and possible solutions read:

"A parent's guide to Educational Reform" by Dan Lips, Jennifer Marshall, and Lindsey Burke, available from the Heritage Foundation.

The U.S. News & World Report examined 21,069 high schools, and rated them with a very complex criteria system. One of the criteria used was "whether the school's least-advantaged students [black, Hispanic, and low-income) were performing better than average for similar students in the state, This is outrages considering blacks and Hispanics the least advantaged, **all** is implied. See my chapter on the media. The report ended with about 100 schools getting a gold rating. These 100 schools had anywhere from 100% to 58.3% of college ready High School students. Can you imagine a school with only 58.3% of their students college ready being given a gold rating? Does this mean that over 20,000 of the schools rated had less than 58% of their students ready for college? The answer is probably yes! If you want something to cry about go on their web site and read the comments about this rating system. They did rank Thomas Jefferson High School number one for the second consecutive year, probably a very good school. We need 21,068 more just like it. They quoted the statistic that out of 30 industrial nations, America ranks 25th in math and 21st in science. They say that economists estimate that the nation's economy would grow by 4.5 percentage points over 20 years if America caught up with the leading nations. We should not just catch up with the leaders we should surpass them big time.

I am including excerpts from the two political parties to show that they give these problems considerable thought. Most of the thought is how can the federal government expend enough money to solve the problem. This is not the way to solve the educational problems. I am hopeful that the readers of this book will get involved and come up with the solutions, that I have missed.

Here is an excerpt from the Democratic 2008 Platform: My comment follows!

A World Class Education for Every Child

In the 21st century, where the most valuable skill is knowledge, countries that out educate us today will out-compete us tomorrow. In the platform hearings, Americans made it clear that it is morally and economically unacceptable that our high-schoolers continue to score lower on math and science tests than most other students in the world and continue to dropout at higher rates than their peers in other industrialized nations. We cannot accept the persistent achievement gap between minority and white students or the harmful disparities that exist between different schools within a state or even a district. Americans know we can and should do better.

The Democratic Party firmly believes that graduation from a quality public school and the opportunity to succeed in college must be the birthright of every child—not the privilege of the few. We must prepare all our students with the 21st century skills they need to succeed by progressing to a new era of mutual responsibility in education. We must set high standards for our children, but we must also hold ourselves accountable—our schools, our teachers, our parents, business leaders, our community and our elected leaders. And we must come together, form partnerships, and commit to providing the resources and reforms necessary to help every child reach their full potential.

Early Childhood

We will make quality, affordable early childhood care and education available to every American child from the day he or she is born. Our Children's First Agenda, including increases in Head Start and Early Head Start, and investments in high-quality Pre-K, will improve quality and provide learning and support to families with children ages zero to five. Our Presidential Early Learning Council will coordinate these efforts.

We must ensure that every student has a high-quality teacher and an effective principal. That starts with recruiting a new generation of teachers and principals by making this pledge—if you commit your life to teaching, America will commit to paying for your college education. We'll provide better preparation, mentoring and career ladders. Where there are teachers who are still struggling and underperforming we should provide them with individual help and support. And if they're still underperforming after that, we should find a quick and fair way—consistent with due process—to put another teacher in that classroom. To reward our teachers, we will follow the lead of school districts and educators that have pioneered innovative ways to increase teacher pay that are developed with teachers, not imposed on them. We will make an unprecedented national investment to provide teachers with better pay and better support to improve their skills, and their students' learning. We'll reward effective teachers who teach in under-served areas, take on added responsibilities like mentoring new teachers, or consistently excel in the classroom.

Higher Education

We believe that our universities, community colleges, and other institutions of higher learning must foster among their graduates the skills needed to enhance economic competitiveness. We will work with institutions of higher learning to produce highly skilled graduates in science, technology, engineering, and math disciplines who will become innovative workers prepared for the 21st century economy.

My Comments:

This agenda, if fully implemented would be almost wonderful even though there are a few problems. However, it just might bankrupt the government. It is very complicated and has something for everyone keeping them indebted to the government. Kiss is the phrase we should use, "Keep it Simple Stupid." The party that wrote this platform is now in power, lets keep an eye on them and see what, if anything, they accomplish. Local control of education will solve most of these problems, if the federal government gets out of the educational business.

Excerpt from the Republican Parties 2008 Platform:

Education Means a More Competitive America

Education is a parental right, a state and local responsibility, and a national strategic interest. Maintaining America's preeminence requires a world-class system of education, with high standards, in which all students can reach their potential. That requires considerable improvement over our current 70 percent high school graduation rate and six-year graduation rate of only 57 percent for colleges. Education is essential to competitiveness, but it is more than just training for the work force of the future. It is through education that we ensure the transmission of a culture, a set of values we hold in common. It has prepared generations for responsible citizenship in a free society, and it must continue to do so. Our party is committed to restoring the civic mission of schools envisioned by the founders of the American public school system. Civic education, both in the classroom and through service learning, should be a cornerstone of American public education and should be central to future school reform efforts.

Principles for Elementary and Secondary Education

All children should have access to an excellent education that empowers them to secure their own freedom and contribute to the betterment of our society. We reaffirm the principles that have been the foundation of the nation's educational progress toward that goal: accountability for student academic achievement; periodic testing on the fundamentals of learning, especially math and reading, history and geography; transparency, so parents and the general public know which schools best serve their students; and flexibility and freedom to innovate so schools and districts can best meet the needs of their students. We advocate policies and methods that are proven and effective: building on the basics, especially phonics; ending social promotion; merit pay for good teachers; classroom discipline; parental involvement; and strong leadership by principals. We reject a one-size-fits-all approach and support parental options, including home schooling, and local innovations such as schools or classes for boys only or for girls only and alternative and innovative school schedules. We recognize and appreciate the importance of innovative education environments, particularly homeschooling, for stimulating academic achievement. We oppose overreaching judicial decisions which deny children access to such environments. We support state efforts to build coordination between elementary and secondary education and higher education such as K-16 councils and dual credit programs. To ensure that all students will have access to the mainstream of American life, we support the English First approach and oppose divisive programs that limit students' future potential. All students must be literate in English, our common language, to participate in the promise of America.

Asserting Family Rights in Schooling

Parents should be able to decide the learning environment that is best for their child. We support choice in education for all families, especially those with children trapped in dangerous and failing schools, whether through charter schools, vouchers or tax credits for attending faith-based or other nonpublic schools, or the option of home schooling. We call for the vigilant enforcement of laws designed to protect family rights and privacy in education. We will energetically assert the right of students to engage in voluntary prayer in schools and to have equal access to school facilities for religious purposes. We renew our call for replacing "family planning" programs for teens with increased funding for abstinence education, which teaches abstinence until marriage as the responsible and expected standard of behavior. Abstinence from sexual activity is the only protection that is 100 percent effective against out-of-wedlock pregnancies and sexually transmitted diseases, including HIV/AIDS when transmitted sexually. We oppose school-based clinics that provide referrals, counseling, and related services for abortion and contraception. Schools should not ask children to answer offensive or intrusive personal nonacademic questionnaires without parental consent. It is not the role of the teacher or school administration to recommend or require the use of psychotropic medications that must be prescribed by a physician.

My Comments:

There are numerous good ideas in this portion of the Republican's Platform, it will be a shame that most will not be implemented. They had their chance and did what? Very little. We, the people, must get involved and encourage the government to implement some of these ideas. Lets do it, now! My ideas are limited, you must have some of your own. Tell your Representative now!

Notes on Education

Chapter Four

What is wrong with America?

Picture: Yourself behind a desk covered with IRS forms.
Picture a large government person behind you with his hands
in your pockets.

The Caption reads:
"The government thinks we just don't pay enough"

The Federal Tax System

The present tax system is the most complex method in the world to collect a fair tax. It is probably close to a million page document and growing, impossible for anyone to fully understand. Experts don't agree on what the rules are, and here we are trying to file our own taxes. The result? Most of us spend thousands of dollars on accountants' fees. Every year the government spends hours creating new tax rules that end up benefiting only a few. The word that comes to mind is "social engineering," not something that benefits the general public.

A much better system would be a consumption tax only. No other type of taxation. This sales type tax would be on all goods and services. It would be a fixed percentage (less other government income) based upon government expenditures, or, better yet, what government expenditures should be. There should be a tax rebate each year based upon personal income. Example: Gross income of less than $30,000 would receive a refund of the exact percentage multiplied by their income. $30,000 to $100,000 would receive a refund of the percentage multiplied by the ratio of their earnings to $30,000. Example: A person with a $40,000 income would receive a rebate of three fourth's of someone earning $30,000. Second example: A person with a $100,000 income would receive a refund of three tenth's of someone earning $30,000 Over $100,000 there would be no rebate. This would tax all spending, even if the money had been earned illegally. This would be a great thing. All increases in the tax rate should require a 75% vote. Alternatively any spending cuts should require only a 40% vote. Here might be a place to quote President Reagan: "The Governments view of the economy can be summed up in a few short phrases: If it moves tax it. If it keeps moving, regulate it, and if it stops moving, subsidize it." We must get away from this mind set. This country and it's people are capable of making the world a fantastic place but only if the government will get out of the way financially and just protect the people from harm.

This consumption tax system would ensure that everyone pays their share, according to their earnings/expenditures. Lower income earners would receive help to allow them to move ahead in this world.

A few more details to help understand the beauty of this plan. A monthly estimated rebate check could be sent to the workers earning less than $50,000, At year end this would be adjusted after total earnings were verified. The government would be able to stimulate the economy very quickly, if required by reducing the tax percentage for limited amount of time. The other possibility would be, reducing the percentage on a particular product or group of products, for a limited time. If the original percentage for the rebate system is maintained everyone would benefit from the stimulation process.

Everything should be taxed at the same rate to keep things simple. This would include housing, both rental and purchased, auto's, boats, airplanes, etc. If financed the interest on the loan would not be taxed. Food, clothing and all necessities would also be taxed. There should be no exceptions. The only way to avoid taxation would be to save. This should encourage savings which would be a good thing. Tax deferrals for retirement plans would not be necessary.

The real problem will be to get this through congress because of the tax lawyers, accountants and others that feed off the present system. Realtors and present tax revenue employee's would be against a consumption type tax. Realtors because of the tax on housing, employees because of possible loss of employment. Fewer employees would be required to manage the consumption tax system versus the present income and other tax systems. This is where the people must be the drivers of this change and make their wishes known.

Businesses need to have exemptions for buying raw materials required for the manufacture of their products. There would be no consumption tax on wages paid or received. Businesses, including corporations, would be treated the same as individuals, except for material and wage exemptions.

In order for the public to know how much tax is being collected, the tax should be added to the price of goods and services, not included in the price.

This tax system would be unfair to tourists to the United States, so, like Canada, we should have a system of reimbursement for most of the tax paid on goods they buy. We must encourage tourism because it is good for our GNP.

It would be my hope that once the federal government changes their tax system, the States would follow. There is no reason that the federal system would not be good for each State. The amount of money saved with one system of taxation would be tremendous. I am recommending the government eliminates all other taxes. No more special interest type of rules, no loop holes. All monies spent will be taxed regardless of whether it was earned legally or illegally. The States should also have a rebate system, I think somewhat simpler. Maybe everyone earning under $30,000 would get the exact percentage back, with a sliding scale to $80,000. Just think no property taxes, special taxes on certain items, (example, phone bills), just one percentage on all items. There would be no tax on items bought for resale. Local taxes could be based on the same principle, I would say with no rebates. It should be a relatively small percentage, besides people could vote with their feet. Well, maybe New York City would not be small but people would still want to live there. Both Parties in their respective Platforms have talked about tax cuts, targeting certain earners and businesses, lets just fix the system now and put everybody on a fair and balanced system.

A portion from the Democratic 2008 Platform

Restoring Fairness to Our Tax Code

We must reform our tax code. It's thousands of pages long, a monstrosity that high-priced lobbyists have rigged with page after page of special interest loopholes and tax shelters. We will shut down the corporate loopholes and tax havens and use the money so that we can provide an immediate middle-class tax cut that will offer relief to workers and their families. We'll eliminate federal income taxes for millions of retirees, because all seniors deserve to live out their lives with dignity and respect. We will not increase taxes on any family earning under $250,000 and we will offer additional tax cuts for middle class families. For families making more than $250,000, we'll ask them to give back a portion of the Bush tax cuts to invest in health care and other key priorities. We will end the penalty within the current Social Security system for public service that exists in several states. We will expand the Earned Income Tax Credit, and dramatically simplify tax filings so that millions of Americans can do their taxes in less than five minutes.

My Comments:

The $250,000 changes will be just more social engineering, but the five minute tax preparation is fantastic, except for the fact that it is only for millions. I want to know will it be for 2 million, less than one percent of the population or for 150 million, one half of the population. My prediction is that five minutes will not happen at all.

When my tax changes and social security changes take place. The American worker will be more productive and less stressed. This will allow for the country to stop all subsidies. Then enter into free trade agreements with all like minded countries.

Notes on Taxation

Chapter Five

What is wrong with America?

Picture: A big house, a beautiful car, a dog, a ride-on lawn mower, three kids and a white picket fence.

The Caption reads:
"The government's dream for us all, whether we work or not."

Financial crisis

The Financial Crisis could be the best thing that ever has happen to the USA.

IF the people of the United States get engaged and knowledgeable about their voting. Vote in people who will solve the problems facing this country. We must eliminate the politicians who have put social engineering ahead of the welfare of the country.

IF the government will take it's responsibility of supervising the various industries seriously. We must use knowledgeable Congress men or women to do this process. The Barney Franks and Chris Dodds of this world must not be in charge of monitoring industries they don't understand. If they did understand what they were creating then they must have used their position for political purposes or social engineering.

IF The various industries and social watch dog agencies must agree that sound business practices should be followed. All compensation should be based on performance, yes, CEO's, you need to be responsible for the outcome of your business.

The present financial crisis needs to be solved but we also need to put everyone, who has contributed to this fiasco, in jail. Perhaps we need a large class action lawsuit against all of these individuals including the government officials and community organizations that promoted and forced banks to make loans to individuals who had no ability to repay them. Bank officials should have been refusing to participate in this debacle but did not do so, therefore, they are also guilty by association. The old saying: "If you are not part of the solution you are part of the problem," applies here. The financial institutions involved in packaging these worthless loans and selling them in the market place under the title of "Collateralized mortgage obligation" are also guilty. They should be hung, drawn and quartered. What were they thinking? There were many people who should have been waving a red flag, why were they not doing it? The banking industry does not seem to have learned anything. They are still promoting credit cards to marginally credit worthy clients. The government never has understood the idea of lending to qualified people. They make loans to country's that will never be able to repay the money. They borrow from the social security fund, (it is not really a fund), with no idea of paying the money back. Just imagine what the government will do with more power, such as ownership in banks, the auto industry, universal healthcare, energy solutions, just to name a few. This prospect scares the hell out of me.

The solution to this problem is very simple, remove the government from private business, and social engineering must stop. Governments can provide guidelines for businesses and good business practices must prevail or be punishable by law. There should be oversight committees that really understand good business practice. We do not need the Barney Franks or Chris Dodds of this world. Acorn, what an idea. It pressures institutions into bad business practices, just for social engineering. Redlining communities, was wrong, but erasing all lines, including common sense, was down right stupid.

Bankers and brokerages must outline their portfolios in their yearly reports and explain why each type of investment is valid. The average investor in these institutions has no idea what a derivative is, or for that matter, what a collateralized mortgage obligation means or what makes a good or bad investment. Warren Buffet's rules for CEO's are simple and remember simple is good. Rule #1

Do not lose any of your shareholders money. Rule #2 Do not forget rule number 1. The CEO of Merrill Lynch said, in early 2008, "It is good for the firm that we've acted so quickly to fix our risk issues. Our capital position is in good shape, and we maintained our high, single-A rating, which is very good for our business. As of the end of 2007, we had a strong liquidity, with about $80 billion in cash available to us. Fundamentally, I think this firm is very sound, and I think that 2008 will be a great year for Merrill Lynch. Of course, the volatile markets and economy at home understandably pose some challenges. I believe that much of the volatility can be offset by the many opportunities in the global marketplace." How can anyone with an eight figure income be so out of touch? This, as I understand it, is typical of what was going on in the financial district. I would hope that by the time this book is published, the major auto companies have declared bankruptcy and have restructured into a viable operation. See the chapter on unions.

Toxic Assets

One way to rid the books of these assets in foreclosure is to call each debt holder in for a review of his liability. Find out how much debt this person or company can handle and then reduce their debt to that amount. The amount of the reduction could be anything from 10 to 60% of the debt. The creditor would then assume this 10 to 60% as their share of the asset. For example: The debt on a house is $200,000 and the debtor can only qualify for a loan of $100,000. He would be allowed to stay in the home and be responsible for a mortgage of $100,000. He would also be responsible for all property taxes and maintenance. The stipulation would be, that in 3 to 7 years the property is to be sold. (The original debtor would have the option of buying it back) Alternatively the proceeds would be divided on a 50/50 basis after any deferred maintenance was paid by the debtor. This allows the banks or lending institutions to have a current loan that is being paid, plus an asset that would be appreciating or depreciating with the market.

The following letter was printed in the Wall Street Journal. It outlines what is happening and who's to blame, I personally don't think they pointed enough fingers, but they were trying to simplify the problem. By limiting the assessment of blame, the public will never really understand what happened. Some things not mentioned were:

Peoples perception that they deserve a house even if they cannot afford to buy one. A liberal idea that has been promoted. The promotion of mortgages to unqualified buyers by lending institutions who knew these mortgages would be bought by Government backed entity's, Fannie and Freddi. Wall street being allowed to create financial instruments that were not backed by credit worthy loans. The absolute gall of this is down right criminal. There is absolutely no reason that proper supervision by Congress should not have stopped this. Unqualified congressional leaders cannot be allowed to supervise industries which they do not understand. This type of supervision is black and white not grey and fuzzy. Anyhow take from the letter what you would see fit.

Dear Main Street: A. Letter of Explanation From Wall Street
By Deal Journal
Thursday, September 18, 2008, provided by WSJ

Dear Main Street,

Are you trying to make sense of what's happening here on Wall Street?

Don't worry — you aren't alone. A lot of people even here are trying to figure that out. It isn't that complicated, but Wall Street is so full of mumbo jumbo that it's easy to get confused — or bored. Say "collateralized mortgage obligation" a dozen times and see if you can stay awake.

More from WSJ.com:
- Getting Reflective About Private Equity and the Financial Crisis

- The Story of How Lehman's Last-Minute Korean Rescue Fell Apart
- The Panic of 2008? What Do We Name the Crisis?

Stick with me, though, Main Street and I'll explain what's going on here in New York.

Believe it or not, you've seen this movie before. And I don't mean, "It's A Wonderful Life," though that movie isn't far from the mark.

What's going on is a classic industry shakeout — not all that different from the shakeout of the American steel or auto industries over the past half century. Just in a much shorter time frame.

In just nine months, we have gone from five big, independent Wall Street brokers to only two — Morgan Stanley and Goldman Sachs.

The government took over Fannie Mae and Freddie Mac, the country's largest mortgage companies, a bit more than a week ago.

And just Tuesday, we nationalized AIG, the world's largest insurer.

Of course, consolidation inevitably produces winners and losers. Lehman Brothers, the fourth largest US broker, is a loser. It went bankrupt two days ago.

Bank of America is a winner. It bought brokerage Merrill Lynch three days ago and is now our nation's largest financial institution.

That's a lot of change in not a lot of time.

And when there's change, there's uncertainty. Today, for example, we still don't know whether Washington Mutual, the largest U.S. savings & loan, will stay independent.

Uncertainty isn't good for any business, as it destroys confidence. It is especially bad for our financial system, because the system runs entirely on confidence. I lend you money confident that you will pay me back. If I don't have confidence in you, I won't lend.

Which is just like Wall Street today. Our nation's financial institutions don't really trust each other. And for good reason.

In all, about $2 trillion dollars of lower quality mortgages are spread about our financial system. Many of these are now in default which threatens the banks that hold them.

And of course the lack of trust spirals. Less lending by banks to each other, less lending to Main Street's companies and less lending to you. In the end, the money's not there for you to get a mortgage or auto loan.

And you account for 70% of the economy. So when the money isn't there, that's bad for everybody. Without credit, you get a crisis — a credit crisis.

Of course, we deserve heaps and heaps of blame. Wall Street took the mortgages, sliced and diced them a hundred ways, sold and traded them. We took a nice cut along the way, blissfully oblivious to the risks.

We do have a remarkable talent for cooking up crazy get-rich schemes. Remember the Internet bubble? That was less than a decade ago.

But Main Street, you're also to blame.

Recall the hundreds of billions in bad mortgages that are now killing Wall Street? That was money lent to you, Main Street, for homes and condos many of you could not afford.

And ironically, it is now your money that will be used to repay those dud mortgages because we on Wall Street are running out of money.

The government takeovers of AIG and Fannie and Freddie? That's your money. J.P. Morgan's buyout of broker Bear Stearns last March was also your money,

You might not like it. We on Wall Street may not like it. And even the politicians in Washington may not like it.

But nobody has a choice — unless you happen to have an odd yearning to live in a barter economy.

So Main Street, our crisis is unfortunately your crisis. We made the mess together and now we pay for it together.

The mergers, government takeovers and bankruptcies that will continue to sweep our financial system are a good sign. It means that we are fixing ourselves. Albeit at gunpoint.

Isn't it strange the way our free market works? The government saves Wall Street — and you Main Street foot the bill.

My advice? Save this letter and show it next time we all embark on another stupid misadventure.

Sincerely, Wall Street

My Comment:

I can only assume this letter will be used quite often, stupid misadventures are our governments method of operation.The next problem to be solved is the National Debt.

I would envision after my social security and taxation plans are in effect the National Debt will take care of itself. My social security and taxation plans will start the ball rolling on growth of the economy and through this growth, tax monies will be available to pay down the Debt. Government spending needs to be addressed. Congress will, after implementing my various plans, have one unfinished task: The task of controlling government spending. I know its a big ask but with our help they can do it. One place to start would be to reduce the number of government employees. Their pay should be comparable to non government employees doing like jobs. No union contracts needed. Do not replace unnecessary employees after they retire. The present elite are the government employees earning wages and benefits far more than comparable employees in the private sector. We need to privatize many of the present government functions. I would see the basic consumption tax rate being reduced by 10% for each 25% reduction in the National Debt. Happy days are just around the corner.

Notes on Financial Problems

Chapter Six

What is wrong with America?

Picture: Our military with their hands tied behind their backs. There's a large United Nations carrying a very small stick which they are pointing at a terrorist.

The Caption reads:
"Everything is going to be all right, you have got to be kidding!"

Military and US involvement in the United Nations

We should have a strong military to protect the US citizens from foreign governments and terrorist organizations, it should also protect our borders from invaders. Recently my grandson told me that he did not agree with the military. Now where did he get this idea, could it be Boston university or one of those liberal schools he has attended, maybe Harvard? We must solve this education stupidity.

A quote from an unknown source:
"War is an ugly thing...but not the ugliest of things; the decayed and degraded state of moral and patriotic feeling which thinks that nothing is worth war is much worse. A man who has nothing for which he is willing to fight and nothing he cares about more than his own personal safety...is a miserable creature who has no chance of being free, unless made and kept so by the exertions of better men than himself."

This is probably a good place to insert this letter written by a "Mohammed at Iraq the Model," a message for Cindy Sheehan:

I realize how tragic your loss is and I know how much pain

there is crushing your heart and I know the darkness that suddenly came to wrap your life and wipe away your dreams and I do feel the heat of your tears that won't dry until you find the answers to your question; why you lost your loved one?

I have heard your story and I understand that you have the full right to ask people to stand by your side and support your cause. At the beginning I told myself, this is yet another woman who lost a piece of her heart and the questions of war, peace and why are killing her everyday. To be frank to you the first thing I thought of was like "why should I listen or care to answer when there are thousands of other women in America, Iraq and Afghanistan who lost a son or a husband or a brother..."

Today I was looking at your picture and I saw in your eyes a persistence, a great pain and a torturing question; why?

I know how you feel Cindy, I lived among the same pains for 35 years but worse than that was the fear from losing our loved ones at any moment. Even while I'm writing these words to you there are feelings of fear, stress, and sadness that interrupt our lives all the time but in spite of all that I'm sticking hard to hope which if I didn't have I would have died years ago.

Ma'am, we asked for your nation's help and we asked you to stand with us in our war and your nation's act was (and still is) an act of ultimate courage and unmatched sense of humanity.

Our request is justified, death was our daily bread and a million Iraqi mothers were expecting death to knock on their doors at any second to claim someone from their families.

Your face doesn't look strange to me at all; I see it everyday on endless numbers of Iraqi women who were struck by losses like yours.

Our fellow country men and women were buried alive, cut to pieces and thrown in acid pools and some were fed to the wild dogs while those who were lucky enough ran away to live like strangers and the Iraqi mother was left to grieve one son buried in an unfound grave and another one living far away who she might not get to see again.

We did nothing to deserve all that suffering, well except for a dream we had; a dream of living like normal people do.

We cried out of joy the day your son and his comrades freed us from the hands of the devil and we went to the streets not believing that the nightmare is over.

We practiced our freedom first by kicking and burning the statues and portraits of the hateful idol who stole 35 years from the life of a nation.

For the first time air smelled that beautiful, that was the smell of freedom.

The mothers went to break the bars of cells looking for the ones they lost 5, 12 or 20 years ago and other women went to dig the land with their bare hand searching for a few bones they can hold in their arms after they couldn't hold them when they belonged to a living person.

I recall seeing a woman on TV two years ago, she was digging through the dirt with her hands. There was no definite grave in there as the whole place was one large grave but she seemed willing to dig the whole place looking for her two brothers who disappeared from earth 24 years ago when they were dragged from their colleges to a chamber of hell.

Her tears mixed with the dirt of the grave and there were journalists asking her about what her brothers did wrong and she was screaming "I don't know, I don't know. They were only college students. They didn't murder anyone, they didn't steal, and they didn't hurt anyone in their lives. All I want to know is the place of their grave."

Why was this woman chosen to lose her dear ones? Why you? Why did a million women have to go through the same pain?

We did not choose war for the sake of war itself and we didn't sacrifice a million lives for fun! We could've accepted our jailor and kept living in our chains for the rest of our lives but it's freedom ma'am.

Freedom is not an American thing and it's not an Iraqi thing, it's what unites us as human beings. We refuse all kinds of restrictions and that's why we fought and still fighting everyday in spite of the swords in the hands of the cavemen who want us dead or slaves for their evil masters.

You are free to go and leave us alone but what am I going to tell your million sisters in Iraq? Should I ask them to leave Iraq too? Should I leave too? What about the eight million who walked through bombs to practice their freedoms and voted? Should they leave this land too?

Is it a cursed land that no one should live in? Why is it that we were chosen to live in all this pain, why me, why my people, why you?

I am not leaving this land because the bad guys are not going to leave us or you to live in peace. They are the same ones who flew the planes to kill your people in New York.

I ask you in the name of God or whatever you believe in; do not waste your son's blood.

We here have decided to avenge humanity, you and all the women who lost their loved ones.

Take a look at our enemy Cindy, look closely at the hooded man holding the sword and if you think he's right then I will back off and support your call.

We live in pain and grief everyday, every hour, every minute; all the horrors of the powers of darkness have been directed at us and I don't know exactly when am I going to feel safe again, maybe in a year, maybe two or even ten; I frankly don't know but I don't want to lose hope and faith.

We are in need for every hand that can offer some help. Please pray for us, I know that God listens to mothers' prayers and I call all the women on earth to pray with you for peace in this world.

Your son sacrificed his life for a very noble cause...No, he sacrificed himself for the most precious value in this existence; that is freedom.

His blood didn't go in vain; your son and our brethren are drawing a great example of selflessness.

God bless his free soul and God bless the souls of his comrades who are fighting evil.

God bless the souls of Iraqis who suffered and died for the sake of freedom.

God bless all the freedom lovers on earth.

My Comment:

Yes, Mohammed you are right, for the value of freedom you must fight, because without it, nothing else matters. We the free people

First Saturday Of Each Month

of this earth should band together and fight for the right to be free. This can be done with a strong world organization.

The United Nations, "What a joke," it is not united in any way. It has never solved a problem of which I am aware, although it has created several. We need to get out of the United Nations and form a union, with like minded people of nations, who want to be free of tyranny. Once this new organization is created we will have some common goals and be able to solve problems such as the mid east conflict and the African continent problems. Our military should not be used in any international conflict without the consent of a large majority of these like minded countries. Exceptions to this would be if our citizens are at risk, or our national interest is at stake. These exceptions need to be tightly defined. Military force should be a last resort solution, but it should be used when necessary. An International organization of like minded Nations will be very powerful in stopping rogue states and leaders, through sanctions, etc.

Furthermore the "World Bank," another joke. This "bank" lends money to countries that have no ability to repay. Aid to countries should not be given as money. Yes, aid should be available to buy necessities, for construction, etc., but not money given to leaders to do as they please. Foreign assistance can sometimes assist in promoting economic growth and development but far more important are a country's economic policies, rule of law, and good governance. Rather than focusing on the level of aid, America should focus its efforts in encouraging developing countries to adopt policies conducive to economic growth and development.

This world should be able to solve all its problems through negotiations, but we must have the big hammer to be able to negotiate with despots and rogue governments or countries.

The war on terror should be expanded to include stopping arms sales to rogue states and organizations. There is no reason that parties like Hamas should have rockets and missiles. We must stop this movement of arms around the world. The people in the Gaza

Strip would be backed by everyone if there was no aggression from them toward Israel. I have always pointed out to people that if you take away all arms from Israel you would have a blood bath on your hands, but if you removed all arms from the Palestinians you would have relative peace.

The Gaza strip problem:

Program after program talk about the humanitarian disaster, which it is, but nobody talks of stopping the continuing Palestinian aggression. The Palestinians must stop firing rockets at Israel, this means stopping arms shipments into Hamas' governing body. We must then help to fix the plight of the Palestinian people. Help them to create their own country, then hold them accountable for any aggression to their neighbors. Israel must then be required to dismantle settlements that encroach into the new country of Palestine.

Both political parties 2008 platforms address "the war on terror." The United States cannot fight this alone. We need the world to fight terror and I do not believe that it can be done through the United Nations. We must either fix the United Nations or get out and start a new world organization that will be united against tyranny. Only then will we be able to put a large portion of the worlds resources towards the fight against terror around the globe.

Notes on the Military and the UN

Chapter Seven

What is wrong with America?

Picture: A hospital emergency ward There are many people headed for the front door....some have sore toes, sore little fingers, or a little headache. Some are just drunk and throwing up. A few have serious conditions that require immediate medical attention. They are working their way through the masses.

The caption reads:
"Low cost healthcare?"

The Health Care System

A couple of questions:

What incentives does the US government have to solve health Care? For every person who dies between 62 and 70 years old the government saves an average of one quarter of a million dollars in social security benefits.

What incentives does big pharmaceuticals have to make people healthy? They sell all their products to sick and unhealthy people.

To start this discussion we must look at the mess in some general terms. The FDA is not looking out for our best interest. The pharmaceutical industry is after nothing but money. Doctors are over worked and tend to get most of there updated information from the pharmaceutical industry. Insurance company's are looking at the financial results. The patients are looking at paying for care with insurance programs with no thought given to cost.

The easy answer to changing the health care system is:

    1)   Separate the FDA from the drug industry.

    2)   Separate the drug industry from Doctors.

3) Separate medical schooling from the drug industry.

4) Create two or three nonprofit health insurance company's to compete with the "for profit" companies.

5) The federal government's rules and regulations on Insurance companies must be reviewed and made user friendly.

6) There should be some rules on how long an employee working for the FDA must wait before going to work for the drug industries, and vise versus. The FDA should design the tests for a new drug, not the drug companies. Nor should the drug companies fund any research for the FDA. There should be oversight of the FDA by government congressional committee, but these oversight committees should be held accountable when things go wrong.

7) There should be no free drug samples given to doctors. Drug companies should not send sales people to doctors for any purpose. Drug sales people recommend their companies drugs to doctors for specific purposes, yet they themselves are not doctors. Drug companies should post their research on web sites so the whole world can evaluate their research and results. Then doctors could evaluate this data and decide which drugs are right for their patients.

8) Teaching future doctors should be about how to heal the body without drugs. The use of drugs should be taught in school, but it should not be the only focus in the treatment of a patient.

9) By far the easiest change in the medical industry to implement, would be to motivate patients to obtain good value for their health care dollars. There needs to be a "wellness care" separate

from a "sick care." There should be incentives for doctors to prevent illness not just treat it. One would think that is part of being a doctor but it's seldom found. Doctors themselves don't know how to stay healthy. It is rare to have a doctor tell one to take this vitamin, supplement or give logical reasons to modify one's diet. People should be motivated to stay healthy, most people don't seem to know how. They have grown up in a system where "if somethings wrong, go get a pill." Doctors are overmedicating their patients, no doubt in my mind. I cannot prove it but I believe my Mother died from doctor prescribed drugs, at age 69.

We rank Twenty-third or so in health care in the world, have you ever ask yourself why? Education both of yourself and the medical field is the simple answer. Recently there was talk about healthy foods being provided in schools, probably too little, hopefully not too late. If you have been in a hospital, you may remember the food as being awful. I remember it as being the worst try at nutrition that I can ever remember. A little about myself: I had a heart attack at age 39 in 1975, spent 18 days in the hospital. The only good thing that came from that stay, besides surviving, was, I quit smoking, on my own with no real pressure or help from the medical staff. Foods: White bread, ice cream, jello, over cooked vegetables, mystery meat, etc. What a way to get well. I went home with medication and suggestions to start some exercise. My first priority was to get off all medications, exercise myself back into shape and start a healthy diet. I read everything I could find about health. There was not much in the medical literature, most of it was available in the underground, produced in the dreaded supplement industry. That industry is where you can find the most valuable health and wellness information today. You will find the national media writing articles about the dangers of most supplements. They are no help at all in educating the public about health.

Life Extension Foundation would be a great consultant to the government in ways to solve the "Health care crisis." Life Extension Foundation has contacted the government with the information about vitamin D and how many lives it would save with supplementation of this inexpensive vitamin. The first thing that would have to happen would be to curtail the lobbyist strangle hold on the elected officials. The FDA needs to be completely overhauled and split into several smaller entities. The pharmaceutical industry and the FDA are in bed with each other, and we need to put an arms length between them. They are stopping some meaningful innovative competition. Medical education needs some adjustments, doctors must learn to treat the person not a disease. Doctors must learn the causes of different diseases and attempt to prevent them. This would be less expensive than having to treat the patients after they have contracted the disease. I dare you to go into a doctors office and when he asks you why you are there, tell him you want to stay healthy, and would like to know how to do it. You most likely will get a blank stare, or at best, a quit smoking, wear your seatbelt and eat a healthy diet. Unless you were born in a vacuum you know seat belts save lives and smoking is bad for you. Even before health care warnings we called cigarettes coffin nails. Healthy diets are different for many people, doctors should be able to give you guidelines.

One possibility to bring down health insurance costs is to start a conservative community investment business. For a dollar a month or so, people could become a partner. This money is invested in the market. This business could then obtain group health insurance rates. All kinds of possibilities exist here, a buyers club for medicines, etc. Keep the business aspect simple so that it will not create problems.

Since it will take time before changes will be made in the health care system, you must take control of your health care. One of the first things you should do is start eating a healthy diet, a couple of the possibilities are, The Mediterranean Diet or better yet is the Calorie Restriction Diet. Both of these diets can be accessed through the internet or several books have been written on these diets. If nothing else you need to stop eating such things as foods containing corn syrup, high fructose corn syrup, partially hydrogenated oils.

Most sugars should be removed from your diet. Get your BMI (body mass index) below 21 if you really want to be healthy or below 25 just to improve your health. Moderate drinking, no smoking, all of these things will reduce your health care costs and you will feel better. If the list of ingredients is lengthy, THINK TWICE! Exercise on some scale would also improve your health, excess exercise is not necessarily healthy. It is imperative that people start taking responsibility for their own health, the savings for a family would be very big indeed.

A little more about myself: Along with a heart attack when I was 39, I had lung cancer when I was 49. One half of my left lung was removed. I take no medications, my BMI is 20.5. I am capable of hiking up to 15 miles or more per day, I am healthy at 73!

My wife was born May 8,1943, she also takes no medications and her BMI is 19.5. Our medical costs are minimal. Most of this good health has been created by reading about health issues and taking supplements.

Notes on Health Care

Chapter Eight

What is wrong with America?

Picture: A map of the United States and Mexico, with the Rio Grande River in between. Thousands of people are swimming towards the States, with one little bus taking people back to Mexico.

The Caption reads:
"Our Immigration Policy"

Immigration Policies

The President of the United States is the person who should take the lead on this important problem. When he swears to uphold the constitution, he promises to protect us from all invaders from foreign soil. There is no reason why the United States Marines along with Border Patrol cannot prevent illegals from crossing our borders.

We must get a handle on this problem, we need a guest worker program with teeth. We also need laws with teeth that will stop employment of illegal workers. They must have a guest work permit or green card. This must be for all workers, even day workers being paid cash. Penalties need to be sufficient to stop all hiring of illegal workers. The government must have a simple guest work permit program that will cover the needs of businesses and households. These guest workers should be able to apply for citizenship and be encouraged to do so legally. It should again become necessary to speak and understand English to become a U.S. Citizen. Criminals should be refused work permits and of course citizenship. Deportation of people who crossed the border illegally should be done with warnings to their Countries of origin. Any illegal crossing into the US should be consider a crime and dealt with accordingly. Everyone who is here illegally should be given three months to apply for a work permit. After that it should be mandatory that all workers either have a work permit, green card or be a citizen.

Notes on Immigration

Chapter Nine

What is wrong with America?

Picture: Three generations of a family gathered around the flat screen television set. There are food stamps strewn on the table along side the cigarettes and beer cans.

The Caption reads:
"Welfare at it's best!"

The Welfare System

The welfare systems of this country should be at the state and local levels not at the federal level.

The welfare system is broken and must be fixed. Generations of families on welfare must be stopped. There must be penalties, not welfare for capable people not working in this world. There should be real incentives for working. Aid should not stop when someone has a low paying job, or a part time job. There should be a sliding scale of some kind. Let's give benefits to the people who are trying. People who start working will become self confident and gain self esteem and will no longer wish to be on welfare.

The present minimum wage rules should not apply to unqualified workers, until they are productive. There should be no free lunch. If nothing else, unemployment benefits or welfare should require some sort of community service. Requiring community service by the unemployed, would stop abuse of the system, where a person works just long enough to qualify for unemployment benefits. This work could be as simple as cleaning streets with a broom, there are many things that would make our world better. The food stamp program should be brought into the modern era with a debit card. This way there could be some control on the type of products. Food stamps should only buy basic food groups not beer, candy, etc. This list should be quite extensive. We need a new system for people who are truly unable to work. This should include housing, health care, skill training, if possible and a total program that will be the envy of the entire free world. These people should not be classified as welfare recipients or be homeless.

Notes on The Welfare System

Chapter Ten

What is wrong with America?

Picture: A fancy car with black windows or a shabby house with a parade of people stopping by.........

The Caption reads:
"Where are the police when you need them?" "These entrepreneurs do not pay taxes!"

The Illegal Drug Problem

The war on drugs is an absolute failure, maybe even worse than that. Some sort of novel approach must be tried. I think that the Government should go into the drug business, the supply side. Sell drugs at police and sheriff stations at one-tenth or less of the cost on the street. The screening of buyers would have to be very intense. Absolutely no first time buyers. Eventually the drug sellers would go out of business, probably in less than a year. The drugs should be in one-time shot quantities and used at the facility, not taken out on the street, except maybe Marihuana. Once the drug dealers are out of business, it should then be possible to reduce the addicts usage with rehabilitation programs, etc.

Notes on Illegal Drugs

Chapter Eleven

What is wrong with America?

Picture: A large person labelled "Lobbyist" with a rope attached to the nose of a Representative who is being lead around.

The Caption reads:
"Our Representatives, working for us?"

Lobbyists

There should be controls on lobbyists, they have too much influence on legislation. Most of the lobbyists power comes from their potential campaign contributions. Perhaps all Lobbying groups should be required to make their donations to a general fund which would be distributed to all Senators and Representative equally. Access to law makers should be limited to group talks on a subject, with written papers distributed to the various media organizations. Free meals, parties and golf outings must stop. There should be several watchdogs examining both sides of the argument. Both interpretations should then be published and made available to the law makers. The amount of pressure lobbyists used to keep Fannie Mae and Freddi Mac away from supervision has recently been revealed, this is downright disgraceful. Lobbying should be a useful education tool but education and pressure are two distinct things. It appears that right now most of the lobbying done is of the pressure type. This needs to be corrected.

Notes on Lobbyists

Chapter Twelve

What is wrong with America?

Picture: The electric and hybrid cars of today with the Presidents seal of approval. Now think about a pile of millions of these large batteries needing to be recycled.

The Caption reads:
"Our energy policy and the resulting toxic waste"

Energy and Carbon Emissions

Technology will take us out of these problems, just surviving the various agendas will be the challenge. I believe that the lowly battery, (a storage device), will be the key to alternative energy. We need batteries that can store a large amount of energy for their size. Households could be run on battery power with solar or wind energy, (when available), used for recharging, alternatively off peak electrically generated power should be used. Batteries are being used to run cars now, but they need to be smaller and hold more energy to really make a difference.

The government needs to create a Manhattan type project to move this technology forward. Once found, it needs to be produced and run by private industry. Another project should be to create a jet type engine that will run on a renewable fuel source. I am sure that creative solutions will be made if the government becomes more industry friendly.

Sound national energy policies must enable America to obtain energy supplies, from a wide range of sources, in a way that is best for the economy. At the same time it must address homeland and national security considerations. An abundant, diverse energy supply is central to America's freedom and prosperity. The principles for an energy strategy that advances freedom and prosperity should emphasize three themes:

Unleashing free enterprise.

1) Protecting America's energy interests.

2) Advancing free global energy markets.

Research and drilling for oil should start in all U.S. controlled territories. These wells need to be capped when oil availability lowers the price then come on line as the price escalates. Clean coal technologies need to be explored and used because this is the low cost fuel for electrical generation. Clean coal technology can and should be sold around the world. Nuclear electrical power generation is necessary in this day of needing all energy sources.

Carbon emissions will also be solved through technology, the government should not regulate this system. The government must treat the carbon emission problem as something that will be solved in the long term, not a crisis with quick fixes. The western world, in the future, will not be viewed as the problem. They will be the leaders in solving the problems. Governments should give incentives to industry not exorbitant penalties. What will happen with an energy tax based on carbon content? It will be put in the general fund then, like most taxes, it will just get used for congressional whims.

We must win the debate on the impact of drilling verses pristine wilderness and oceans. We can have both. If we do not drill we will not get pristine wilderness or oceans, because someone else will drill. The world is run on oil and it will not be denied. We need to participate because we will do it better.

Bio fuels could be good but should not be subsidized. Growing basic food products for fuel has numerous pitfalls, not the least of which could be creating food shortages around the world. This would be solving a very minor portion, of a major problem, but creating another. Subsidies are social engineering solutions to programs gone crazy. The only type of subsidies that make sense are ones to help develop a product. The battery solution, would be an example and could be used to help solve the energy problem. The government should let industry take over production. The government should be compensated for the development either by a licensing scheme or payment program.

The space program is a good example of passing along scientific breakthroughs for commercial purposes.

Notes on Energy and Carbon Emissions

Chapter Thirteen

What is wrong with America?

Picture: A laughing Al Gore, smoking a big cigar, surrounded by a big pile of money. He is on the porch of his huge house, looking over his large private airplane and his little bitty electric car.

The Caption reads:
"Wow! There is so much money to be made in this global warming stuff"

Climate Change

Climate change has got to be the most outrageous hoax of all time. Yes, there is climate change and there has been since the world began. Man, no doubt, is causing some of the change, but when I read about how much is attributed to Man, I start to come unglued. The last ice age was some 20,000 years ago and the world has been warming ever since.

On Senator James Inhofe's blog, there is a summary of this year's news that might make one skeptical of man-made global warming. It includes a report that there are over 650 international scientists who can be counted as doubters.

Scaring children in school so that they run home and demand that the household start recycling is criminal. Al Gore is #18 on Bernard Goldberg's "100 people who are screwing up America." He spends more energy capital in promoting his stupid cause than most extended families spend in a life time. Maybe not so stupid, he is becoming rich promoting this theory. If you think you have a recycling problem now, just wait. The financial crisis has the government involved in the auto industry and they will mandate electric cars. When these autos need to be recycled with their huge batteries, that will be a crisis. Electric autos should progress slowly until the ultimate battery has been designed.

Proponents of propping up failing automakers at taxpayer expense so that they can continue to pay out on excessively generous union contracts should take note: That policy has been tried before. The British government did it in the late 1970s, when the company British Leyland ran into trouble because it failed to make cars that consumers wanted. Despite government "investment" of more than £1.4 billion into the company between 1979 and 1983, British Leyland was eventually broken up and sold off. The government had feared the loss of employment, that would result from British Leyland's collapse, but the end of the story suggests that the best employment policy is to let the market find the most profitable use of resources.

In the 1800's, in London, you needed to cut the air with a knife to see across the street. What changed that situation was the coming of the oil age, which reduced the burning of wood and coal. The oil age is at its peak now and will be replaced slowly by newer and less damaging energy sources, without government mandates. Even third world countries don't want to live with pollution. China's Olympics accentuated that. Such things as inhalers for asthmatics have been banned. They were very effective and have been replaced with less effective ones. These are just a couple of examples of "Climate change fanatics," gone amok. I am not a scientist but I will tell you that the biggest item and I do mean biggest, by a huge margin, that contributes to climate change, is our Sun. Man cannot do anything about it. "Climate change fanatics" should start working on projects that will improve overall human conditions. Yes, we should recycle, just like we should pick up litter, because it is the right thing to do. Replacing incandescent light bulbs with ones that contain mercury, making them an environmental hazard, was the epitome of stupidity. If you want a good fictional read try Michael Crighton's: "State of Fear." It conveys my thoughts about the "global warming crowd."

Notes on Climate Change

Chapter Fourteen

What is wrong with America?

Picture: Several large union thugs in their large cars talking about getting the next big union contract for government workers.

The Caption reads:
"Who are they working for?" "Be honest you already know."

Unions

Have you ever ask yourself why the unions donate millions of their workers hard earned dollars to election coffers? These donations do not benefit their workers in any monetary way or in any societal way. I believe the real reason is to improve the union managements power structure. The other question that comes to mind, is, why are they pushing for non-secret ballots? The answer is easy they cannot win certain types of elections without peer and thug type pressure.

The unions have passed their sell by date. When unions first began, they were necessary and beneficial to the working public. Then, industry was abusing workers, by paying low wages without benefits. The hours were long and working conditions abominable, just to name a few problems. In today's climate these types of problems will not occur without being rectified through the courts or investigative journalism. Unions have become a self serving entity. Almost all contributions to political parties were to the democratic party without a vote of the membership. Brain washing would be how I would describe their tactics for convincing the membership that the democratic party is the only party looking after their interests. Describing the Democratic party as the working class party, would be one of their slogans. They would describe the republican party being the party of the rich. Can people not see that rich democrats are in office and many of the rich people are major supporters of the democratic party. George Soros and Warren Buffet come to mind along with the Hollywood crowd. The reason is that the really rich have had better luck pressuring the democratic party for loop holes in the tax structures. Some of the really rich feel guilty about their successes, maybe they were lucky or just born to the right parents. They have been conditioned to believe that the democratic party is the only party for the down trodden.

Unions have pressured businesses into contracts that good business models cannot sustain, auto makers for example. Unions have created a pay scale based on seniority not performance and have created unrealistic pension plans. It is almost impossible to fire an ineffective employee. Corruption has also occurred in union management. The union dues collected have been used for things that have nothing to do with improving employee conditions.

Teachers unions have not helped the good teachers or students. They have created a management system, along with government involvement, that is destroying the educational system. A good teacher could go anywhere and earn good money if they didn't have to join a union. Ineffective teachers need to be removed from the system and unions make this very difficult.

What is the purpose of Government unions? It allows employees to be promoted beyond their competence level. Unions dictate to the government their requirements for their members. There are negotiations which can result in "slow downs," or "strikes" The resultant chaos often forces the government to accept the union's demands. One thing the unions have done for government workers is to get them out of the social security system and into a better (although still a Ponzi scheme) pension system. This must end, everyone should be on the same page, see my social security system solution, Chapter Two.

Unions have created expected retirement plans that will be in effect after 20 years of work or at 55 years of age. This puts big pressure on businesses and government to fulfill these expectations. Yes, this is possible but the worker has to make this happen through savings, investments or other methods. The social security pension plan and many other pension plans are of the Ponzi type. If you don't know what a Ponzi scheme is look it up. Auto Companies, governments and others are depending on present employees to pay for past employee's pensions. This works quite well when life expectancy is 60, but today it is approaching 85 and in the future 100+. These schemes then self destruct. If you think the present system is good, I have a chain letter you must invest in.

My thinking about unions has changed a little because of information a friend shared with me. Unions do have their place if run by the employees. It is the professionally run unions that are the problem because they become self serving entices.

Another note from the internet

Get Your Union Data Now

Starting next year, union members will have an even better picture of how their union dues are being spent. The Department of Labor has recently completed new rules requiring union-controlled trusts to file financial disclosure forms. The disclosures for union-controlled trusts complement the disclosure requirements already established for unions.

How will union transparency fare with a new Congress and incoming Obama administration? One of the major accomplishments of the Department of Labor under Secretary Elaine Chao was to create UnionReports.gov, an easy-to-use online database of spending by unions.

At UnionReports.gov, you can learn, for instance, that the Service Employees International Union gave Planned Parenthood $10,000 in 2007.

While rolling back reporting requirements is unlikely, there is no guarantee that adequate funding will be provided for the Web site to continue. Without the Web site it would be harder to get the data from the union's financial disclosure forms. The department is working hard to make sure it has a strong audience for UnionReports.gov, which would make it harder to kill the project.

If you are interested in union accountability, you might want to grab as much data as you can, while the site is still up. Also, increasing traffic for the site wouldn't hurt the case for continuing the effort.

First Saturday Of Each Month

Notes on Unions

Chapter Fifteen

What is wrong with America?

Picture: A major news room. The headlines read: "The worst economy ever." "Recession is coming." "The best economy ever." The boss is saying: "How can we best manipulate the masses today?"

The Caption reads:
"Who is going to make up the news today?"

The Media

The existing newspaper business is most likely on its last hurrah, we can only hope. Bias in news reporting has no place in the free world. Maybe the New York times and papers like them should move to Russia, China or Venezuela. The time is right for a newspaper printing "Nothing but the Truth," which would hopefully become the newspaper of choice.

There are some real opportunities, it seems that the public would support an investigative print media. Subjects are numerous, Politicians, Legislation, Financial instruments, Public figures, the various wars, the drug culture, Prisons, Hollywood's agenda, or anyone with an agenda. Not to mention education with all its problems, health care and pharmaceuticals, with their business ethics. Lobbyists, with all their ramifications for promoting various laws. A daily or weekly newspaper that had integrity, no heresy or third party information that had not been investigated, would be a success.

It is important that the general public has accurate information so that they are able to vote with intelligence. Yes, you could have editorial comments, but I would suggest guest editorial writers from both sides of the spectrum. Come on somebody step up and start what could be an instant winner. If only I was younger and had a journalistic background, I would love to put out this type of publication. A good place to start would be an expose' on the ACLU. Another subject could be Bernard Goldberg's: "100 people who are screwing up America." There are hundreds who have been left off that list. All inconsistencies in political public speaking should be acknowledged and exposed. Double standards in any media outlet should be exposed for what it is, just commentary. One subject that should be investigated until the truth comes out are the agendas of big foundations, the Ford Foundation for one, but I am sure there are several others. Another subject that needs to be exposed is the greed in corporate executives. Yes, they deserve salaries commensurate with their performance, but corruption or freeloading off the companies should be exposed.

A good media would uncover the weaknesses of the politicians who are entrenched in "safe seats." It is absolutely obscene that they are continually reelected. All funding issues should be above board and those that aren't should be exposed by a good media. Two examples are the funding of ACLU and PETA. The media should expose teachers that subscribe to Ann Pelo's book: "Thats not Fair," which is a teachers guide to activism with young children. Any Documentaries need to be challenged if they distort the truth. Health is another area where a good media could make a huge difference in what is truth and what is fiction. Welfare fraud could be an on going column, the possibilities are unlimited. Come on somebody make a fortune, just do it.

Notes on the Media

Chapter Sixteen

What could be right with America?

Picture: Our Founding Father's sitting around a table discussing the Constitution. One of them is saying: "I think we have covered everything." "Everyone should read it."

The Caption reads:
"Now is the time just do it!"

Constitution of the United States

If you have never read the constitution now is a good time. The roots of liberty and our laws are based in Philadelphia, the birthplace of the Declaration of Independence and the U.S. Constitution. It is the law of the United States. What is a constitution? It is the form of government, delineated by the mighty hand of the people, in which certain first principles of fundamental law is established. The Constitution is fixed and certain, it contains the permanent will of the people, and is the supreme law of the land. It is paramount to the power of the Legislature, and can be revoked or altered only by the authority that made it. The constitution contains the instructions from the sovereign people of the United States of America and any interpreter should discover what that instruction is and apply it as the situation demands. Legislators are elected to make laws that are intended to serve the public good and operate within constitutional limits. The President is elected to secure the national interest and to insure that those laws are implemented effectively. Judges are not elected for the general purpose of making good policy. Judges are selected to interpret and apply the law in the cases and controversies that arise before them. The American constitution was not meant to be a constitution of precedents, it is a constitution of "first principle." The Constitution does not depend on the passions or parties of the time, but will remain the same yesterday, today and forever. The constitution is supreme law because it was ratified by the sovereign people in convention, and it alone authorizes and limits government actions. As the constitution is legislated by the most authoritative body within the political system, all other legislation is inferior to that law and void if contradictory to it. To start your further reading about the constitution, may I recommend The book: "The Heritage Guide to the Constitution," also "How to read the constitution" by Keith E. Whittington.

I have put the Constitution in the body of the book instead of, as an appendix because it is essential that we read it to understand the importance of the power of the people. I understand that this is going to be a tough assignment. Every time I read it I get some new information.

Provided by USConstitution.net

(Note: Repealed text is not noted in this version. Spelling errors have been corrected in this version. For an uncorrected, annotated version of the Constitution, visit http://www.usconstitution.net/const.html)

We the People of the United States, in Order to form a more perfect Union, establish Justice, insure domestic Tranquility, provide for the common defence, promote the general Welfare, and secure the Blessings of Liberty to ourselves and our Posterity, do ordain and establish this Constitution for the United States of America.

Article 1.
Section 1
All legislative Powers herein granted shall be vested in a Congress of the United States, which shall consist of a Senate and House of Representatives.

Section 2
The House of Representatives shall be composed of Members chosen every second Year by the People of the several States, and the Electors in each State shall have the

Qualifications requisite for Electors of the most numerous Branch of the State Legislature.

No Person shall be a Representative who shall not have attained to the Age of twenty five Years, and been seven Years a Citizen of the United States, and who shall not, when elected, be an Inhabitant of that State in which he shall be chosen.

Representatives and direct Taxes shall be apportioned among the several States which may be included within this Union, according to their respective Numbers, which shall be determined by adding to the whole Number of free Persons, including those bound to Service for a Term of Years, and excluding Indians not taxed, three fifths of all other Persons.

The actual Enumeration shall be made within three Years after the first Meeting of the Congress of the United States, and within every subsequent Term of ten Years, in such Manner as they shall by Law direct. The Number of Representatives shall not exceed one for every thirty Thousand, but each State shall have at Least one Representative; and until such enumeration shall be made, the State of New Hampshire shall be entitled to choose three, Massachusetts eight, Rhode Island and Providence Plantations one, Connecticut five, New York six, New Jersey four, Pennsylvania eight, Delaware one, Maryland six, Virginia ten, North Carolina five, South Carolina five and Georgia three.

When vacancies happen in the Representation from any State, the Executive Authority thereof shall issue Writs of Election to fill such Vacancies.

The House of Representatives shall choose their Speaker and other Officers; and shall have the sole Power of Impeachment.

Section 3

The Senate of the United States shall be composed of two Senators from each State, chosen by the Legislature thereof, for six Years; and each Senator shall have one Vote.

Immediately after they shall be assembled in Consequence of the first Election, they shall be divided as equally as may be into three Classes. The Seats of the Senators of the first Class shall be vacated at the Expiration of the second Year, of the second Class at the Expiration of the fourth Year, and of the third Class at the Expiration of the sixth Year, so that one third may be chosen every second Year; and if Vacancies happen by Resignation, or otherwise, during the Recess of the Legislature of any State, the Executive thereof may make temporary Appointments until the next Meeting of the Legislature, which shall then fill such Vacancies.

No person shall be a Senator who shall not have attained to the Age of thirty Years, and been nine Years a Citizen of the United States, and who shall not, when elected, be an Inhabitant of that State for which he shall be chosen.

The Vice President of the United States shall be President of the Senate, but shall have no Vote, unless they be equally divided.

The Senate shall choose their other Officers, and also a President pro tempore, in the absence of the Vice President, or when he shall exercise the Office of President of the United States.

The Senate shall have the sole Power to try all Impeachments. When sitting for that Purpose, they shall be on Oath or Affirmation. When the President of the United States is tried, the Chief Justice shall preside: And no Person shall be convicted without the Concurrence of two thirds of the Members present.

First Saturday Of Each Month

Judgment in Cases of Impeachment shall not extend further than to removal from Office, and disqualification to hold and enjoy any Office of honor, Trust or Profit under the United States: but the Party convicted shall nevertheless be liable and subject to Indictment, Trial, Judgment and Punishment, according to Law.

Section 4

The Times, Places and Manner of holding Elections for Senators and Representatives, shall be prescribed in each State by the Legislature thereof; but the Congress may at any time by Law make or alter such Regulations, except as to the Place of Choosing Senators.

The Congress shall assemble at least once in every Year, and such Meeting shall be on the first Monday in December, unless they shall by Law appoint a different Day.

Section 5

Each House shall be the Judge of the Elections, Returns and Qualifications of its own Members, and a Majority of each shall constitute a Quorum to do Business; but a smaller number may adjourn from day to day, and may be authorized to compel the Attendance of absent Members, in such Manner, and under such Penalties as each House may provide.

Each House may determine the Rules of its Proceedings, punish its Members for disorderly Behavior, and, with the Concurrence of two-thirds, expel a Member.

Each House shall keep a Journal of its Proceedings, and from time to time publish the same, excepting such Parts as may in their Judgment require Secrecy; and the Yeas and Nays of the Members of either House on any question shall, at the Desire of one fifth of those Present, be entered on the Journal.

Neither House, during the Session of Congress, shall, without the Consent of the other, adjourn for more than three days, nor to any other Place than that in which the two Houses shall be sitting.

Section 6
The Senators and Representatives shall receive a Compensation for their Services, to be ascertained by Law, and paid out of the Treasury of the United States. They shall in all Cases, except Treason, Felony and Breach of the Peace, be privileged from Arrest during their Attendance at the Session of their respective Houses, and in going to and returning from the same; and for any Speech or Debate in either House, they shall not be questioned in any other Place.

No Senator or Representative shall, during the Time for which he was elected, be appointed to any civil Office under the Authority of the United States which shall have been created, or the Emoluments whereof shall have been increased during such time; and no Person holding any Office under the United States, shall be a Member of either House during his Continuance in Office.

Section 7
All bills for raising Revenue shall originate in the House of Representatives; but the Senate may propose or concur with Amendments as on other Bills.

Every Bill which shall have passed the House of Representatives and the Senate, shall, before it become a Law, be presented to the President of the United States; If he approve he shall sign it, but if not he shall return it, with his Objections to that House in which it shall have originated, who shall enter the Objections at large on their Journal, and proceed to reconsider it. If after such Reconsideration two thirds of that House shall agree to pass the Bill, it shall be sent, together with the Objections, to the other House, by which it shall likewise be reconsidered, and if approved by two thirds of that House, it shall become a Law. But in all such Cases the Votes of both Houses shall be determined by Yeas and Nays, and the Names of the Persons voting for and against the Bill shall be entered on the Journal of each House respectively. If any Bill shall not be returned by the President within ten Days (Sundays excepted) after it shall have been presented to him, the Same shall be a Law, in like Manner as if he had signed it, unless the Congress by their Adjournment prevent its Return, in which Case it shall not be a Law.

Every Order, Resolution, or Vote to which the Concurrence of the Senate and House of Representatives may be necessary (except on a question of Adjournment) shall be presented to the President of the United States; and before the Same shall take Effect, shall be approved by him, or being disapproved by him, shall be repassed by two thirds of the Senate and House of Representatives, according to the Rules and Limitations prescribed in the Case of a Bill.

Section 8
The Congress shall have Power To lay and collect Taxes, Duties, Imposts and Excises, to pay the Debts and provide for the common Defence and general Welfare of the United States; but all Duties, Imposts and Excises shall be uniform throughout the United States;

To borrow money on the credit of the United States;

To regulate Commerce with foreign Nations, and among the several States, and with the Indian Tribes;

To establish an uniform Rule of Naturalization, and uniform Laws on the subject of Bankruptcies throughout the United States;

To coin Money, regulate the Value thereof, and of foreign Coin, and fix the Standard of Weights and Measures;

To provide for the Punishment of counterfeiting the Securities and current Coin of the United States;

To establish Post Offices and Post Roads;

To promote the Progress of Science and useful Arts, by securing for limited Times to Authors and Inventors the exclusive Right to their respective Writings and Discoveries;

To constitute Tribunals inferior to the supreme Court;

To define and punish Piracies and Felonies committed on the high Seas, and Offenses against the Law of Nations;

To declare War, grant Letters of Marque and Reprisal, and make Rules concerning Captures on Land and Water;

To raise and support Armies, but no Appropriation of Money to that Use shall be for a longer Term than two Years;

To provide and maintain a Navy;

To make Rules for the Government and Regulation of the land and naval Forces;

To provide for calling forth the Militia to execute the Laws of the Union, suppress Insurrections and repel Invasions;

To provide for organizing, arming, and disciplining the Militia, and for governing such Part of them as may be employed in the Service of the United States, reserving to the States respectively, the Appointment of the Officers, and the Authority of training the Militia according to the discipline prescribed by Congress;

To exercise exclusive Legislation in all Cases whatsoever, over such District (not exceeding ten Miles square) as may, by Cession of particular States, and the acceptance of Congress, become the Seat of the Government of the United States, and to exercise like Authority over all Places purchased by the Consent of the Legislature of the State in which the Same shall be, for the Erection of Forts, Magazines, Arsenals, dock-Yards, and other needful Buildings; And To make all Laws which shall be necessary and proper for carrying into Execution the foregoing Powers, and all other Powers vested by this Constitution in the Government of the United States, or in any Department or Officer thereof.

Section 9

The Migration or Importation of such Persons as any of the States now existing shall think proper to admit, shall not be prohibited by the Congress prior to the Year one thousand eight hundred and eight, but a tax or duty may be imposed on such Importation, not exceeding ten dollars for each Person.

The privilege of the Writ of Habeas Corpus shall not be suspended, unless when in Cases of Rebellion or Invasion the public Safety may require it.

No Bill of Attainder or ex post facto Law shall be passed.

No capitation, or other direct, Tax shall be laid, unless in Proportion to the Census or Enumeration herein before directed to be taken.

No Tax or Duty shall be laid on Articles exported from any State.

No Preference shall be given by any Regulation of Commerce or Revenue to the Ports of one State over those of another: nor shall Vessels bound to, or from, one State, be obliged to enter, clear, or pay Duties in another.

No Money shall be drawn from the Treasury, but in Consequence of Appropriations made by Law; and a regular Statement and Account of the Receipts and Expenditures of all public Money shall be published from time to time.

No Title of Nobility shall be granted by the United States: And no Person holding any Office of Profit or Trust under them, shall, without the Consent of the Congress, accept of any present, Emolument, Office, or Title, of any kind whatever, from any King, Prince or foreign State.

Section 10
No State shall enter into any Treaty, Alliance, or Confederation; grant Letters of Marque and Reprisal; coin Money; emit Bills of Credit; make any Thing but gold and silver Coin a Tender in Payment of Debts; pass any Bill of Attainder, ex post facto Law, or Law impairing the Obligation of Contracts, or grant any Title of Nobility.

No State shall, without the Consent of the Congress, lay any Imposts or Duties on Imports or Exports, except what may be absolutely necessary for executing its inspection Laws: and the net Produce of all Duties and Imposts, laid by any State on Imports or Exports, shall be for the Use of the Treasury of the United States; and all such Laws shall be subject to the Revision and Control of the Congress.

No State shall, without the Consent of Congress, lay any duty of Tonnage, keep Troops, or Ships of War in time of Peace, enter into any Agreement or Compact with another State, or with a foreign Power, or engage in War, unless actually invaded, or in such imminent Danger as will not admit of delay.

Article 2.
Section 1
The executive Power shall be vested in a President of the United States of America. He shall hold his Office during the

Term of four Years, and, together with the Vice-President chosen for the same Term, be elected, as follows:

Each State shall appoint, in such Manner as the Legislature thereof may direct, a Number of Electors, equal to the whole Number of Senators and Representatives to which the State may be entitled in the Congress: but no Senator or Representative, or Person holding an Office of Trust or Profit under the United States, shall be appointed an Elector.

The Electors shall meet in their respective States, and vote by Ballot for two persons, of whom one at least shall not lie an Inhabitant of the same State with themselves. And they shall make a List of all the Persons voted for, and of the Number of Votes for each; which List they shall sign and certify, and transmit sealed to the Seat of the Government of the United States, directed to the President of the Senate. The President of the Senate shall, in the Presence of the Senate and House of Representatives, open all the Certificates, and the Votes shall then be counted. The Person having the greatest Number of Votes shall be the President, if such Number be a Majority of the whole Number of Electors appointed; and if there be more than one who have such Majority, and have an equal Number of Votes, then the House of Representatives shall immediately choose by Ballot one of them for President; and if no Person have a Majority, then from the five highest on the List the said House shall in like Manner choose the President. But in choosing the President, the Votes shall be taken by States, the Representation from each State having one Vote; a quorum for this Purpose shall consist of a Member or Members from two-thirds of the States, and a Majority of all the States shall be necessary to a Choice. In every Case, after the Choice of the President, the Person having the greatest Number of Votes of the Electors shall be the Vice President. But if there should remain two or more who have equal Votes, the Senate shall choose from them by Ballot the Vice-President.

First Saturday Of Each Month

The Congress may determine the Time of choosing the Electors, and the Day on which they shall give their Votes; which Day shall be the same throughout the United States.

No person except a natural born Citizen, or a Citizen of the United States, at the time of the Adoption of this Constitution, shall be eligible to the Office of President; neither shall any Person be eligible to that Office who shall not have attained to the Age of thirty-five Years, and been fourteen Years a Resident within the United States.

In Case of the Removal of the President from Office, or of his Death, Resignation, or Inability to discharge the Powers and Duties of the said Office, the same shall devolve on the Vice President, and the Congress may by Law provide for the Case of Removal, Death, Resignation or Inability, both of the President and Vice President, declaring what Officer shall then act as President, and such Officer shall act accordingly, until the Disability be removed, or a President shall be elected.

The President shall, at stated Times, receive for his Services, a Compensation, which shall neither be increased nor diminished during the Period for which he shall have been elected, and he shall not receive within that Period any other Emolument from the United States, or any of them. Before he enter on the Execution of his Office, he shall take the following Oath or Affirmation:

"I do solemnly swear (or affirm) that I will faithfully execute the Office of President of the United States, and will to the best of my Ability, preserve, protect and defend the Constitution of the United States."

Section 2
The President shall be Commander in Chief of the Army and Navy of the United States, and of the Militia of the

several States, when called into the actual Service of the United States; he may require the Opinion, in writing, of the principal Officer in each of the executive Departments, upon any subject relating to the Duties of their respective Offices, and he shall have Power to Grant Reprieves and Pardons for Offenses against the United States, except in Cases of Impeachment.

He shall have Power, by and with the Advice and Consent of the Senate, to make Treaties, provided two thirds of the Senators present concur; and he shall nominate, and by and with the Advice and Consent of the Senate, shall appoint Ambassadors, other public Ministers and Consuls, Judges of the supreme Court, and all other Officers of the United States, whose Appointments are not herein otherwise provided for, and which shall be established by Law: but the Congress may by Law vest the Appointment of such inferior Officers, as they think proper, in the President alone, in the Courts of Law, or in the Heads of Departments.

The President shall have Power to fill up all Vacancies that may happen during the Recess of the Senate, by granting Commissions which shall expire at the End of their next Session.

Section 3
He shall from time to time give to the Congress Information of the State of the Union, and recommend to their Consideration such Measures as he shall judge necessary and expedient; he may, on extraordinary Occasions, convene both Houses, or either of them, and in Case of Disagreement between them, with Respect to the Time of Adjournment, he may adjourn them to such Time as he shall think proper; he shall receive Ambassadors and other public Ministers; he shall take Care that the Laws be faithfully executed, and shall Commission all the Officers of the United States.

Section 4
The President, Vice President and all civil Officers of the United States, shall be removed from Office on Impeachment for, and Conviction of, Treason, Bribery, or other high Crimes and Misdemeanors.

Article 3.
Section 1
The judicial Power of the United States, shall be vested in one supreme Court, and in such inferior Courts as the Congress may from time to time ordain and establish. The Judges, both of the supreme and inferior Courts, shall hold their Offices during good Behavior, and shall, at stated Times, receive for their Services a Compensation which shall not be diminished during their Continuance in Office.

Section 2
The judicial Power shall extend to all Cases, in Law and Equity, arising under this Constitution, the Laws of the United States, and Treaties made, or which shall be made, under their Authority; to all Cases affecting Ambassadors, other public Ministers and Consuls; to all Cases of admiralty and maritime Jurisdiction; to Controversies to which the United States shall be a Party; to Controversies between two or more States; between a State and Citizens of another State; between Citizens of different States; between Citizens of the same State claiming Lands under Grants of different States, and between a State, or the Citizens thereof, and foreign States, Citizens or Subjects.

In all Cases affecting Ambassadors, other public Ministers and Consuls, and those in which a State shall be Party, the supreme Court shall have original Jurisdiction. In all the other Cases before mentioned, the supreme Court shall have appellate Jurisdiction, both as to Law and Fact, with such Exceptions, and under such Regulations as the Congress shall make.

The Trial of all Crimes, except in Cases of Impeachment, shall be by Jury; and such Trial shall be held in the State where the said Crimes shall have been committed; but when not committed within any State, the Trial shall be at such Place or Places as the Congress may by Law have directed.

Section 3
Treason against the United States, shall consist only in levying War against them, or in adhering to their Enemies, giving them Aid and Comfort. No Person shall be convicted of Treason unless on the Testimony of two Witnesses to the same overt Act, or on Confession in open Court.

The Congress shall have power to declare the Punishment of Treason, but no Attainder of Treason shall work Corruption of Blood, or Forfeiture except during the Life of the Person attainted.

Article 4.
Section 1
Full Faith and Credit shall be given in each State to the public Acts, Records, and judicial Proceedings of every other State. And the Congress may by general Laws prescribe the Manner in which such Acts, Records and Proceedings shall be proved, and the Effect thereof.

Section 2
The Citizens of each State shall be entitled to all Privileges and Immunities of Citizens in the several States. A Person charged in any State with Treason, Felony, or other Crime, who shall flee from Justice, and be found in another State, shall on demand of the executive Authority of the State from which he fled, be delivered up, to be removed to the State having Jurisdiction of the Crime.

No Person held to Service or Labour in one State, under the Laws thereof, escaping into another, shall, in Consequence of any Law or Regulation therein, be discharged from such

Service or Labour, But shall be delivered up on Claim of the Party to whom such Service or Labour may be due.

Section 3
New States may be admitted by the Congress into this Union; but no new States shall be formed or erected within the Jurisdiction of any other State; nor any State be formed by the Junction of two or more States, or parts of States, without the Consent of the Legislatures of the States concerned as well as of the Congress.

The Congress shall have Power to dispose of and make all needful Rules and Regulations respecting the Territory or other Property belonging to the United States; and nothing in this Constitution shall be so construed as to Prejudice any Claims of the United States, or of any particular State.

Section 4
The United States shall guarantee to every State in this Union a Republican Form of Government, and shall protect each of them against Invasion; and on Application of the Legislature, or of the Executive (when the Legislature cannot be convened) against domestic Violence.

Article 5.
The Congress, whenever two thirds of both Houses shall deem it necessary, shall propose Amendments to this Constitution, or, on the Application of the Legislatures of two thirds of the several States, shall call a Convention for proposing Amendments, which, in either Case, shall be valid to all Intents and Purposes, as part of this Constitution, when ratified by the Legislatures of three fourths of the several States, or by Conventions in three fourths thereof, as the one or the other Mode of Ratification may be proposed by the Congress; Provided that no Amendment which may be made prior to the Year One thousand eight hundred and eight shall in any Manner affect the first and fourth Clauses in the Ninth Section of the first Article; and that no State,

without its Consent, shall be deprived of its equal Suffrage in the Senate.

Article 6.
All Debts contracted and Engagements entered into, before the Adoption of this Constitution, shall be as valid against the United States under this Constitution, as under the Confederation.

This Constitution, and the Laws of the United States which shall be made in Pursuance thereof; and all Treaties made, or which shall be made, under the Authority of the United States, shall be the supreme Law of the Land; and the Judges in every State shall be bound thereby, any Thing in the Constitution or Laws of any State to the Contrary notwithstanding.

The Senators and Representatives before mentioned, and the Members of the several State Legislatures, and all executive and judicial Officers, both of the United States and of the several States, shall be bound by Oath or Affirmation, to support this Constitution; but no religious Test shall ever be required as a Qualification to any Office or public Trust under the United States.

Article 7.
The Ratification of the Conventions of nine States, shall be sufficient for the Establishment of this Constitution between the States so ratifying the Same.

Done in Convention by the Unanimous Consent of the States present the Seventeenth Day of September in the Year of our Lord one thousand seven hundred and Eighty seven and of the Independence of the United States of America the Twelfth. In Witness whereof We have hereunto subscribed our Names.

George Washington - President and deputy from Virginia

New Hampshire - John Langdon, Nicholas Gilman

Massachusetts - Nathaniel Gorham, Rufus King

Connecticut - William Samuel Johnson, Roger Sherman

New York - Alexander Hamilton

New Jersey - William Livingston, David Brearley, William Paterson, Jonathan Dayton

Pennsylvania - Benjamin Franklin, Thomas Mifflin, Robert Morris, George Clymer, Thomas Fitzsimons, Jared Ingersoll, James Wilson, Gouvernour Morris

Delaware - George Read, Gunning Bedford Jr., John Dickinson, Richard Bassett, Jacob Broom

Maryland - James McHenry, Daniel of St Thomas Jenifer, Daniel Carroll

Virginia - John Blair, James Madison Jr.

North Carolina - William Blount, Richard Dobbs Spaight, Hugh Williamson

South Carolina - John Rutledge, Charles Cotesworth Pinckney, Charles Pinckney, Pierce Butler

Georgia - William Few, Abraham Baldwin

Attest: William Jackson, Secretary

Amendment 1
Congress shall make no law respecting an establishment of religion, or prohibiting the free exercise thereof; or abridging the freedom of speech, or of the press; or the

right of the people peaceably to assemble, and to petition the Government for a redress of grievances.

Amendment 2

A well regulated Militia, being necessary to the security of a free State, the right of the people to keep and bear Arms, shall not be infringed.

Amendment 3

No Soldier shall, in time of peace be quartered in any house, without the consent of the Owner, nor in time of war, but in a manner to be prescribed by law.

Amendment 4

The right of the people to be secure in their persons, houses, papers, and effects, against unreasonable searches and seizures, shall not be violated, and no Warrants shall issue, but upon probable cause, supported by Oath or affirmation, and particularly describing the place to be searched, and the persons or things to be seized.

Amendment 5

No person shall be held to answer for a capital, or otherwise infamous crime, unless on a presentment or indictment of a Grand Jury, except in cases arising in the land or naval forces, or in the Militia, when in actual service in time of War or public danger; nor shall any person be subject for the same offense to be twice put in jeopardy of life or limb; nor shall be compelled in any criminal case to be a witness against himself, nor be deprived of life, liberty, or property, without due process of law; nor shall private property be taken for public use, without just compensation.

Amendment 6

In all criminal prosecutions, the accused shall enjoy the right to a speedy and public trial, by an impartial jury of the State and district wherein the crime shall have been committed, which district shall have been previously ascertained by law, and to be informed of the nature and cause of the accusation; to be confronted with the witnesses against him; to have compulsory process for obtaining witnesses in his favor, and to have the Assistance of Counsel for his defence.

Amendment 7
In Suits at common law, where the value in controversy shall exceed twenty dollars, the right of trial by jury shall be preserved, and no fact tried by a jury, shall be otherwise re-examined in any Court of the United States, than according to the rules of the common law.

Amendment 8
Excessive bail shall not be required, nor excessive fines imposed, nor cruel and unusual punishments inflicted.

Amendment 9
The enumeration in the Constitution, of certain rights, shall not be construed to deny or disparage others retained by the people.

Amendment 10
The powers not delegated to the United States by the Constitution, nor prohibited by it to the States, are reserved to the States respectively, or to the people.

Amendment 11
The Judicial power of the United States shall not be construed to extend to any suit in law or equity, commenced or prosecuted against one of the United States by Citizens of another State, or by Citizens or Subjects of any Foreign State.

Amendment 12
The Electors shall meet in their respective states, and vote by ballot for President and Vice-President, one of whom, at least, shall not be an inhabitant of the same state with

themselves; they shall name in their ballots the person voted for as President, and in distinct ballots the person voted for as Vice-President, and they shall make distinct lists of all persons voted for as President, and of all persons voted for as Vice-President and of the number of votes for each, which lists they shall sign and certify, and transmit sealed to the seat of the government of the United States, directed to the President of the Senate;

The President of the Senate shall, in the presence of the Senate and House of Representatives, open all the certificates and the votes shall then be counted;

The person having the greatest Number of votes for President, shall be the President, if such number be a majority of the whole number of Electors appointed; and if no person have such majority, then from the persons having the highest numbers not exceeding three on the list of those voted for as President, the House of Representatives shall choose immediately, by ballot, the President. But in choosing the President, the votes shall be taken by states, the representation from each state having one vote; a quorum for this purpose shall consist of a member or members from two-thirds of the states, and a majority of all the states shall be necessary to a choice. And if the House of Representatives shall not choose a President whenever the right of choice shall devolve upon them, before the fourth day of March next following, then the Vice-President shall act as President, as in the case of the death or other constitutional disability of the President.

The person having the greatest number of votes as Vice-President, shall be the Vice-President, if such number be a majority of the whole number of Electors appointed, and if no person have a majority, then from the two highest numbers on the list, the Senate shall choose the Vice-President; a quorum for the purpose shall consist of two-thirds of the whole number of Senators, and a majority of the whole number shall be necessary to a choice. But no person constitutionally ineligible to the office of President shall be eligible to that of Vice-President of the United States.

Amendment 13
1. Neither slavery nor involuntary servitude, except as a punishment for crime whereof the party shall have been duly convicted, shall exist within the United States, or any place subject to their jurisdiction.

2. Congress shall have power to enforce this article by appropriate legislation.

Amendment 14
1. All persons born or naturalized in the United States, and subject to the jurisdiction thereof, are citizens of the United States and of the State wherein they reside. No State shall make or enforce any law which shall abridge the privileges or immunities of citizens of the United States; nor shall any State deprive any person of life, liberty, or property, without due process of law; nor deny to any person within its jurisdiction the equal protection of the laws.

2. Representatives shall be apportioned among the several States according to their respective numbers, counting the whole number of persons in each State, excluding Indians not taxed. But when the right to vote at any election for the choice of electors for President and Vice-President of the United States, Representatives in Congress, the Executive and Judicial officers of a State, or the members of the Legislature thereof, is denied to any of the male inhabitants of such State, being twenty-one years of age, and citizens of the United States, or in any way abridged, except for participation in rebellion, or other crime, the basis of representation therein shall be reduced in the proportion which the number of such male citizens shall bear to the

whole number of male citizens twenty-one years of age in such State.

3. No person shall be a Senator or Representative in Congress, or elector of President and Vice-President, or hold any office, civil or military, under the United States, or under any State, who, having previously taken an oath, as a member of Congress, or as an officer of the United States, or as a member of any State legislature, or as an executive or judicial officer of any State, to support the Constitution of the United States, shall have engaged in insurrection or rebellion against the same, or given aid or comfort to the enemies thereof. But Congress may by a vote of two-thirds of each House, remove such disability.

4. The validity of the public debt of the United States, authorized by law, including debts incurred for payment of pensions and bounties for services in suppressing insurrection or rebellion, shall not be questioned. But neither the United States nor any State shall assume or pay any debt or obligation incurred in aid of insurrection or rebellion against the United States, or any claim for the loss or emancipation of any slave; but all such debts, obligations and claims shall be held illegal and void.

5. The Congress shall have power to enforce, by appropriate legislation, the provisions of this article.

Amendment 15
1. The right of citizens of the United States to vote shall not be denied or abridged by the United States or by any State on account of race, color, or previous condition of servitude.

2. The Congress shall have power to enforce this article by appropriate legislation.

First Saturday Of Each Month

Amendment 16
The Congress shall have power to lay and collect taxes on incomes, from whatever source derived, without apportionment among the several States, and without regard to any census or enumeration.

Amendment 17
The Senate of the United States shall be composed of two Senators from each State, elected by the people thereof, for six years; and each Senator shall have one vote. The electors in each State shall have the qualifications requisite for electors of the most numerous branch of the State legislatures.

When vacancies happen in the representation of any State in the Senate, the executive authority of such State shall issue writs of election to fill such vacancies: Provided, That the legislature of any State may empower the executive thereof to make temporary appointments until the people fill the vacancies by election as the legislature may direct.

This amendment shall not be so construed as to affect the election or term of any Senator chosen before it becomes valid as part of the Constitution.

Amendment 18
1. After one year from the ratification of this article the manufacture, sale, or transportation of intoxicating liquors within, the importation thereof into, or the exportation thereof from the United States and all territory subject to the jurisdiction thereof for beverage purposes is hereby prohibited.

2. The Congress and the several States shall have concurrent power to enforce this article by appropriate legislation.

3. This article shall be inoperative unless it shall have been ratified as an amendment to the Constitution by

the legislatures of the several States, as provided in the Constitution, within seven years from the date of the submission hereof to the States by the Congress.

Amendment 19
The right of citizens of the United States to vote shall not be denied or abridged by the United States or by any State on account of sex. Congress shall have power to enforce this article by appropriate legislation.

Amendment 20
1. The terms of the President and Vice President shall end at noon on the 20th day of January, and the terms of Senators and Representatives at noon on the 3d day of January, of the years in which such terms would have ended if this article had not been ratified; and the terms of their successors shall then begin.

2. The Congress shall assemble at least once in every year, and such meeting shall begin at noon on the 3d day of January, unless they shall by law appoint a different day.

3. If, at the time fixed for the beginning of the term of the President, the President elect shall have died, the Vice President elect shall become President. If a President shall not have been chosen before the time fixed for the beginning of his term, or if the President elect shall have failed to qualify, then the Vice President elect shall act as President until a President shall have qualified; and the Congress may by law provide for the case wherein neither a President elect nor a Vice President elect shall have qualified, declaring who shall then act as President, or the manner in which one who is to act shall be selected, and such person shall act accordingly until a President or Vice President shall have qualified.

4. The Congress may by law provide for the case of the

death of any of the persons from whom the House of Representatives may choose a President whenever

the right of choice shall have devolved upon them, and for the case of the death of any of the persons from whom the Senate may choose a Vice President whenever the right of choice shall have devolved upon them.

5. Sections 1 and 2 shall take effect on the 15th day of October following the ratification of this article.

6. This article shall be inoperative unless it shall have been ratified as an amendment to the Constitution by the legislatures of three-fourths of the several States within seven years from the date of its submission.

Amendment 21
1. The eighteenth article of amendment to the Constitution of the United States is hereby repealed.

2. The transportation or importation into any State, Territory, or possession of the United States for delivery or use therein of intoxicating liquors, in violation of the laws thereof, is hereby prohibited.

3. The article shall be inoperative unless it shall have been ratified as an amendment to the Constitution by conventions in the several States, as provided in the Constitution, within seven years from the date of the submission hereof to the States by the Congress.

Amendment 22
1. No person shall be elected to the office of the President more than twice, and no person who has held the office of President, or acted as President, for more than two years of a term to which some other person was elected President shall be elected to the office of the President more than once. But this Article shall not apply to any person holding

the office of President, when this Article was proposed by the Congress, and shall not prevent any person who may be holding the office of President, or acting as President, during the term within which this Article becomes operative from holding the office of President or acting as President during the remainder of such term.

2. This article shall be inoperative unless it shall have been ratified as an amendment to the Constitution by the legislatures of three-fourths of the several States within seven years from the date of its submission to the States by the Congress.

Amendment 23
1. The District constituting the seat of Government of the United States shall appoint in such manner as the Congress may direct: A number of electors of President and Vice President equal to the whole number of Senators and Representatives in Congress to which the District would be entitled if it were a State, but in no event more than the least populous State; they shall be in addition to those appointed by the States, but they shall be considered, for the purposes of the election of President and Vice President, to be electors appointed by a State; and they shall meet in the District and perform such duties as provided by the twelfth article of amendment.

2. The Congress shall have power to enforce this article by appropriate legislation.

Amendment 24
1. The right of citizens of the United States to vote in any primary or other election for President or Vice President, for electors for President or Vice President, or for Senator or Representative in Congress, shall not be denied or abridged by the United States or any State by reason of failure to pay any poll tax or other tax.

2. The Congress shall have power to enforce this article by appropriate legislation.

Amendment 25
1. In case of the removal of the President from office or of his death or resignation, the Vice President shall become President.

2. Whenever there is a vacancy in the office of the Vice President, the President shall nominate a Vice President who shall take office upon confirmation by a majority vote of both Houses of Congress.

3. Whenever the President transmits to the President pro tempore of the Senate and the Speaker of the House of Representatives his written declaration that he is unable to discharge the powers and duties of his office, and until he transmits to them a written declaration to the contrary, such powers and duties shall be discharged by the Vice President as Acting President.

4. Whenever the Vice President and a majority of either the principal officers of the executive departments or of such other body as Congress may by law provide, transmit to the President pro tempore of the Senate and the Speaker of the House of Representatives their written declaration that the President is unable to discharge the powers and duties of his office, the Vice President shall immediately assume the powers and duties of the office as Acting President.

Thereafter, when the President transmits to the President pro tempore of the Senate and the Speaker of the House of Representatives his written declaration that no inability exists, he shall resume the powers and duties of his office unless the Vice President and a majority of either the principal officers of the executive department or of such other body as Congress may by law provide, transmit within four days to the President pro tempore of the Senate and the Speaker of the House of Representatives their written declaration that the President is unable to discharge the powers and duties of his office. Thereupon Congress shall decide the issue, assembling within forty eight hours for that purpose if not in session. If the Congress, within twenty one days after receipt of the latter written declaration, or, if Congress is not in session, within twenty one days after Congress is required to assemble, determines by two thirds vote of both Houses that the President is unable to discharge the powers and duties of his office, the Vice President shall continue to discharge the same as Acting President; otherwise, the President shall resume the powers and duties of his office.

Amendment 26
1. The right of citizens of the United States, who are eighteen years of age or older, to vote shall not be denied or abridged by the United States or by any State on account of age.

2. The Congress shall have power to enforce this article by appropriate legislation.

Amendment 27
No law, varying the compensation for the services of the Senators and Representatives, shall take effect, until an election of Representatives shall have intervened.

Notes on the Constitution

Chapter Seventeen

What is wrong with America?

Picture: A large man with a whip. There are starving kids and dogs around his feet.

The Caption reads:
"A liberals view of a conservative"

Some of my conservative thoughts and the ten conservative principles from Russell Kirk

I believe in Limited government, especially at the federal level. Governing principles work best when the rules and regulations are locally controlled. The military and any dealings with Foreign governments should be at the federal level. State disputes and companies that do commerce across State lines should be regulated by the federal government. Most things that effect the everyday life of individuals should be locally controlled.

We need a strong military to protect the people of the USA from foreign invasion, which would also include illegal border crossings.

Taxation should be at a minimum, just enough for a well run limited government.

Protect the citizens from religious persecution, freedom of speech, and all the amendments in the constitution.

Protect the People's right to bear arms. There can be limited rules on the type of arms, but the right to bear arms is part of the Constitution. Criminals have lost this and other rights.

Govern by using the Constitution, it's amendments, and the Bill of Rights.

I believe a strong moral order must prevail in a civilized society, this means everyone knows right from wrong and they have strong convictions about justice and honor. Religion has always been the leader in moral order and that is why our governing principles have a religious background. Even atheists know that stealing is wrong. Leaders of our communities, governing bodies and industry must be the role models. Very strong penalties should be imposed on these leaders that stray from moral responsibilities. Now would be a good time to send a message to these leaders in the financial industry.

The following is the best analysis of Conservatism and its Principles that I have ever read.

Ten Conservative Principles

By Russell Kirk

Being neither a religion nor an ideology, the body of opinion termed conservatism possesses no holy writ and no Das Kapital to provide dogmata. So far as it is possible to determine what conservatives believe, the first principles of the conservative persuasion are derived from what leading conservative writers and public men have professed during the past two centuries. After some introductory remarks on this general theme, I will proceed to list ten such conservative principles.

A witty presidential candidates of recent times, Mr. Eugene McCarthy remarked a few months ago that nowadays he employs the word "liberal" as an adjective merely. That renunciation of "liberal" as a noun of politics, a partisan or ideological tag, is some measure of the triumph of the conservative mentality during the 1980s—including the triumph of the conservative side of Mr. McCarthy's own mind and character.

Perhaps it would be well, most of the time, to use this word "conservative" as an adjective chiefly. For there exists no Model Conservative, and conservatism is the negation of ideology: it is a state of mind, a type of character, a way of looking at the civil social order.

In essence, the conservative person is simply one who finds the permanent things more pleasing that Chaos and Old Night, (Yet conservatives know, with Burke, that healthy "change is the means of our preservation.") A people's historic continuity of experience, says the conservative, offers a guide to policy far better than the abstract designs of coffee-house philosophers. But of course there is more to the conservative persuasion than this general attitude.

It is not possible to draw up a neat catalogue of conservatives' convictions; nevertheless, I offer you, summarily, ten general principles; it seems safe to say that most conservatives would subscribe to most of these maxims. In various editions of my book The Conservative Mind I have listed certain canons of conservative thought—the list differing somewhat from edition to edition; in my anthology The Portable Conservative Reader I offer variations upon this theme. Today I present to you a summary of conservative assumptions differing somewhat from my canons in those two books of mine. In fine, the diversity of ways in which conservative views may find expression is itself proof that conservatism is no fixed ideology. What particular principles conservatives emphasize during any given time will vary with the circumstances and necessities of that era. The following ten articles of belief reflect the emphases of conservatives in America nowadays.

First, the conservative believes that there exists an enduring moral order. That order is made for man, and man is made for it: human nature is a constant, and moral truths are permanent.

This word order signifies harmony. There are two aspects or types of order: the inner order of the soul and the outer order of the commonwealth. Twenty-five centuries ago, Plato taught this doctrine, but even the educated nowadays find it difficult to understand. The problem of order has been a principal concern of conservatives ever since conservative became a term of politics.

Our twentieth century world has experienced the hideous consequences of the collapse of belief in a moral order. Like the atrocities and disasters of Greece in the fifth century before Christ, the ruin of great nations in our century shows us the pit into which fall societies that mistake clever self-interest, or ingenious social controls, for pleasing alternatives to an oldfangled moral order.

It has been said by liberal intellectuals that the conservative believes all social questions, at heart, to be questions of private morality. Properly understood, this statement is quite true. A society in which men and women are governed by belief in an enduring moral order, by a strong sense of right and wrong, by personal convictions about justice and honor, will be a good society—whatever political machinery it may utilize; while a society in which men and women are morally adrift, ignorant of norms, and intent chiefly upon gratification of appetites, will be a bad society—no matter how many people vote and no matter how liberal its formal constitution may be. For confirmation of the latter argument, we have merely to glance about us in the District of Columbia.

Second, the conservative adheres to custom, convention, and continuity. It is old custom that enables people to live together peaceably; the destroyers of custom demolish more than they know or desire. It is through convention—a word much abused in our time—that we contrive to avoid perpetual disputes about rights and duties: law at base is a body of conventions. Continuity is the means of linking generation to generation; it matters as much for society as it does for the individual; without it, life is meaningless. When successful revolutionaries have effaced old customs, derided old conventions, and broken the continuity of social institutions—why, presently they discover the necessity of establishing fresh customs, conventions, and continuity; but that process is painful and slow; and the new social order that eventually emerges may be much inferior to the old order that radicals overthrew in their zeal for the Earthly Paradise.

Conservatives are champions of custom, convention, and continuity because they prefer the devil they know to the devil they do not know. Order and justice and freedom, they believe, are the artificial products of a long social experience, the result of centuries of trial and reflection and sacrifice. Thus the body social is a kind of spiritual corporation, comparable to the church; it may even be called a community of souls. Human society is no machine to be treated mechanically. The continuity, the life blood, of a society must not be interrupted. Burke's reminder of the necessity for prudent change is in the mind of the conservative. But necessary change, conservatives argue, ought to be gradual and discriminatory, never unfixing old interests at once.

Third, conservatives believe in what may be called the principle of prescription. Conservatives sense that modern people are dwarfs on the shoulders of giants, able to see farther than their ancestors only because of the great stature of those who have preceded us in time. Therefore conservatives very often emphasize the importance of prescription—that is, of things established by immemorial usage, so that the mind of man runneth not to the contrary. There exist rights of which the chief sanction is their antiquity—including rights to property, often. Similarly, our morals are prescriptive in great part. Conservatives argue that we are unlikely, we moderns, to make perilous to weigh every passing issue on the basis of private judgement and private rationality. The individual is foolish, but the species is wise, Burke declared. In politics we do well to abide by precedent and precept and even prejudice, for the great mysterious incorporation of the human race has acquired a prescriptive wisdom far greater than any man's petty private rationality.

Fourth,conservatives are guided by their principle of prudence. Burke agrees with Plato that in the statesman, prudence is chief among virtues. Any public measure ought to be judged by its Probable long run consequences, not merely by temporary advantage or popularity. Liberals and radicals, the conservative says, are imprudent: for they dash at their objectives without giving heed to the risk of new abuses worse than the evils they hope to sweep away. As John Randolph of Roanoke put it. Providence moves slowly, but the devil always hurries. Human society being complex, remedies cannot be simple if they are to be efficacious. The conservative declares that he acts only after sufficient reflection, having weighed the consequences. Sudden and slashing reforms are as perilous as sudden and slashing surgery.

Fifth, conservatives pay attention to the principle of variety. They feel affection for the proliferating intricacy of long established social institutions and modes of life, as distinguished from the narrowing uniformity and deadening egalitarianism of radical systems. For the preservation of a healthy diversity in any civilization, there must survive orders and classes, differences in material condition, and many sorts of inequality. The only true forms of equality at the Last judgement and equality before a just court of law; all other attempts at leveling must lead, at best, to social stagnation. Society requires honest and able leadership; and if natural and institutional differences are destroyed, presently some tyrant or host of squalid oligarchs will create new forms of inequality.

Sixth, conservatives are chastened by their principle of imperfectibility. Human nature suffers irremediably from certain grave faults, the conservatives know. Man being imperfect, no perfect social order ever can be created. Because of human restlessness, mankind would grow rebellious order any utopian domination, and would break out once more in violent discontent—or else expire of boredom. To seek for utopia is to end in disaster, the conservative says: we are not made for perfect things. All that we reasonably can expect is a tolerable ordered, just, and free society, in which some evils, maladjustments, and suffering will continue to lurk. By proper attention to prudent reform, we may preserve and improve this tolerable order. But if the old institutional and moral safeguards of a nation are neglected, then the anarchic impulse in humankind breaks loose: "the ceremony of innocence is drowned." The ideologues who promise the perfection of man and society have converted a great part of the twentieth century world into a terrestrial hell.

Seventh, conservatives are persuaded that freedom and property are closely linked. Separate property from private possession, and Leviathan becomes master of all. Upon the foundation of private property, great civilizations are built. The more widespread is the possession of private property, the more stable and productive is a commonwealth. Economic leveling, conservatives maintain, is not economic progress. Getting and spending are not the chief aims of human existence; but a sound economic basis for the person, the family, and the commonwealth is much to be desired.

Sir Henry Maine, in his Village Communities, puts strongly the case for private property: "Nobody is at liberty to attack several property and to say at the same time that he values civilization. The history of the two cannot be disentangled." For the institution of several property— that is, private property—has been a powerful instrument for teaching men and women responsibility, for providing motives to integrity, for supporting general culture, for raising mankind above the level of mere drudgery, for affording leisure to think and freedom to act. To be able to retain the fruits of one's labor; to be able to see one's work made permanent; to be able to bequeath one's property to one's posterity; to be able to rise from the natural condition of grinding poverty to the security of enduring accomplishment; to have something that is really one's own—these are advantages difficult to deny. The conservative acknowledges that the possession of property fixes certain duties upon the possessor; he accepts those moral and legal obligations cheerfully.

Eighth, conservatives uphold voluntary community, quite as they oppose involuntary collectivism. Although Americans have been attached strongly to privacy and private rights, they also have been a people conspicuous for a successful spirt of community. In a genuine community, the decisions most directly affecting the lives of citizens are made locally and voluntarily. Some of these functions are carried out by local political bodies, others by private associations: so long as they are kept local, and are marked by the general agreement of those affected, they constitute healthy community. But when these functions pass by default or usurpation to centralized authority, then community is in serious danger. Whatever is beneficent and prudent in modern democracy is made possible through cooperative volition. If then, in the name of an abstract democracy, the functions of community are transferred to distant political direction—why, real government by the consent of the governed gives way to a standardizing process hostile to freedom and human dignity.

For a nation is no stronger than the numerous little communities of which it is composed. A central administration, or a corps of select managers and civil servants, however well intentioned and well trained, cannot confer justice and prosperity and tranquility upon a mass of men and women deprived of their old responsibilities. That experiment has been made before; and it has been disastrous. It is the performance of our duties in community that teaches us prudence and efficiency and charity.

Ninth, the conservative perceives the need for prudent restraints upon power and upon human passions. Politically speaking, power is the ability to do as one likes, regardless of the wills of one's fellows. A state in which an individual or a small group are able to dominate the wills of their fellows without check is a despotism, whether it is called monarchical or aristocratic or democratic. When every person claims to be a power unto himself, then society falls into anarchy. Anarchy never lasts long, being intolerable for everyone, and contrary to the ineluctable fact that some persons are more strong and more clever than their neighbors. To anarchy there succeeds tyranny or oligarchy, in which power is monopolized by a very few. The conservative endeavors to so limit and balance political power that anarchy or tyranny may not arise, in every age, nevertheless, men and women are tempted to overthrow the limitations upon power, for the sake of some fancied temporary advantage. It is characteristic of the radical that he thinks of power as a force for good—so long as the power falls into his hands. In the name of liberty, the French and Russian revolutionaries abolished the old restraints upon power, but power cannot be abolished; it always finds its way into someone's hands. That power which the revolutionaries had thought oppressive in the hands of the old regime became many times as tyrannical in the hands of the radical new masters of the state.

Knowing human nature for a mixture of good and evil, the conservative does not put his trust in mere benevolence. Constitutional restrictions, political checks and balances, adequate enforcement of the laws, the old intricate web-of restraints upon will and appetite—these the conservative approves as instruments of freedom and order. A just government maintains a healthy tension between the claims of authority and the claims of liberty.

Tenth, the thinking conservative understands-that permanence and change must be recognized and reconciled in a vigorous society. The conservative is not opposed to social improvement, although he doubts whether there is any such force as a mystical Progress, with a Roman P, at work in the world. When a society is progressing in some respects, usually it is declining in other respects. The conservative knows that any healthy society is influenced by two forces, which Samuel Taylor Coleridge called its Permanence and its Progression. The Permanence of a society is formed by those enduring interests and convictions that give us stability and continuity; without that Permanence, the fountains of the great deep are broken up, society slipping into anarchy. The Progression in society is that spirit and that body of talents which urge us on to prudent reforms and improvement; without that Progression, a people stagnate. Therefore the intelligent conservative endeavors to reconcile the claims of Permanence and the claims of Progression. He thinks that the liberal and the radical, blind to the just claims of Permanence, would endanger the heritage bequeathed to us, in: an endeavor to hurry us into some dubious Terrestrial Paradise. The conservative, in short, favors reasoned and temperate progress; he is opposed to the cult of Progress, whose votaries believe that everything new necessarily is superior to everything old.

Change is essential to the body social, the conservative reasons, just as it is essential to the human body. A body that has ceased to renew itself has begun to die. But if that body is to be vigorous, the change must occur in a regular manner, harmonizing with the form and nature of that body; otherwise change produces a monstrous growth, a cancer, which devours its host. The conservative takes care that nothing in a society should ever be wholly old, and that nothing should ever be wholly new. This is the means of the conservation of a nation, quite as it is the means of conservation of a living organism. Just how much change a society requires, and what sort of change, depend upon the circumstances of an age and a nation.

Such, then, are ten principles that have loomed large during the two centuries of modern conservative thought. Other principles of equal importance might have been discussed here: the conservative understanding of justice, for one, or the conservative view of education. But such subjects, time running on, I must leave to your private investigation.

Who affirms those ten conservative principles nowadays? In practical politics, commonly a body of general convictions is linked with a body of interests. Marxists argue, indeed, that professed political principle is a mere veil for advancement of the economic interests of a class or faction: that is, no real principle exists—merely ideology. Such is not my view: but we ought to recognize connections between political doctrines and social or economic interest groups, when such connections exist; they may be innocent enough, or they may make headway at the expense of the general public interest. What interest or group of interests back the conservative element in American politics?

That question is not readily answered. Many rich Americans endorse liberal or radical causes; affluent suburbs frequently vote for liberal men and measures; attachment to conservative sentiments does not follow the line that Marxist analysts of politics expect to find. The owners of small properties, as a class, tend to be more conservative than do the possessors of much property (this latter often in the abstract form of stocks and bonds). One may remark that most conservatives hold religious convictions; yet the officers of mainline Protestant churches, together with church bureaucracies, frequently ally themselves with radical organizations; while some curious political affirmations have been heard recently among the Catholic hierarchy. Half a century ago, it might have been said that most college professors were conservative; that could not be said truthfully today; yet physicians, lawyers, dentists, and other professional people—or most of them—subscribe to conservative journals and generally vote for persons they take to be conservative candidates.

In short, the conservative interest appears to transcend the usual classification of most American voting blocs according to wealth, age, ethnic origin, religion, occupation, education, and the like. If we may speak of a conservative interest, this appears to be the interest bloc of people concerned for stability: those citizens who find the pace of change to swift, the loss of continuity and permanence too painful, the break with the American past too brutal, the damage to community dismaying, the designs of innovators' imprudent and inhumane. Certain material interests are bound up with this resistance to insensate change: nobody relishes having his savings reduced to insignificance by inflation of the currency. But the moving power behind the renewed conservatism of the American public is not some scheme of personal or corporate aggrandizement; rather, it is the impulse for survival of a culture that wakes to its peril near the end of the twentieth century. We might well call militant conservatives the Party of the Permanent Things. Perhaps no words have been more abused, both in the popular press and within the Academy, than conservatism and conservative. The New York Times, not without malice prepense, now and again refers to Stalinists within the Soviet Union as conservatives. Silly anarchistic tracts, under the label libertarian, are represented in some quarters as conservative publications—this in the United States of America, whose Constitution is described by Sir Henry Maine as the most successful device in the history of politics! Even after more than three decades of the renewal of conservative thought in this land, it remains necessary to make it clear to the public that conservatives are not merely folk content with the dominations and power of the moment; nor anarchists in disguise who would pull down, if they could, both the political and the moral order; nor persons for whom the whole of life is the accumulation of money, like so many Midases.

Therefore it is of importance to know whereof one speaks, and not to mistake the American conservative impulse for some narrow and impractical ideology. If the trumpet give an uncertain sound, who shall go forth to battle? For intellectual development, the first necessity is to define one's terms. If we can enlarge the understanding of conservatism;s first principles, we will have begun a reinvigoration of the conservative imagination. The great line of demarcation in modern politics, Eric Voegelin used to point out, is not a division between liberals on one side and totalitarians on the other. No, on one side of that line are those men and women who fancy that the temporal order is the only order, and that material needs are there only needs, and that they may do as they like with human patrimony. On the other side of that line are all those people who recognize an enduring moral order in the universe, a constant human nature, and high duties toward the order spiritual and the order temporal.

Conservatives cannot offer America the fancied Terrestrial Paradise that always, in reality, has turned out to be an Earthly Hell. What they can offer is politics as the art of the possible; and an opportunity to stand up for that old lovable human nature; and conscious participation in the defense of order and justice and freedom. Unlike liberals and radicals, conservatives even indulge in prayer, let the Supreme Court say what it may.

This general description of basic assumptions by conservatives I have thrust upon you, ladies and gentlemen, in the hope of persuading you to think upon these things at your leisure, for the Republic's sake. Conceivably I may have succeeded in rousing some tempers and some hopes. Pax vobiscum.

Notes on Conservative Principles

Chapter Eighteen

Conservative and Common Sense ideas that make the world a better place

I believe that every one is created equal and should be treated as such. Color blindness is essential to have a better world. Such things as the Black Caucus should not exist, this is not color blindness. Before you call me a racist, you should know a few things about me. My favorite political personality is a black woman, my favorite actor is a black man, (he supports Obama) my all time favorite football player is a black man. One of my favorite all time baseball players is a black man, my favorite supreme court justice is a black man, I could go on, but you get the idea. In my extended family I have two lovely black great nieces. When I was in the army stationed in Texas from 1955 to 1957 I had six close friends and one was black. We had to do such things as sneak him into the drive-in movies, (Blacks were not permitted). I would have voted for Obama if he thought like me.

Tocqueville wrote that there are three reasons for a nations success: "Its material circumstances, its laws, and its 'mores,' that is, its moral habits and customs." These moral habits and customs are deteriorating rapidly and the country and its people need to get them under control. People pressure could do wonders.

I believe that people should abide by the laws of the country, crime of any sort should be punished according to the crime.

I believe that gays should have all the same rights as everyone else. The problem is the word "marriage." It is used to describe a union between a man and a woman and has been for centuries. The general public should never allow it to be otherwise. Gays should be able to form a union between any two people and have all the same rights as a married couple except, call it any other word in the world's languages. Now here's a challenge for someone: Come up with that word and win a place in history.

I believe that there should be some decency in Music, Movies Television and Books. I understand free speech and you can say "fuck" as many times as you want but for what purpose? Certainly not to make the world a better place. Similarly, the interactive video games that are anti-everything. What is the purpose? It's certainly does not improve the world. Maybe we could set another day aside to protest the film, music and television industries. The third Saturday of each month meet at the various offices of these businesses. We can and should take an active part in solving this problem of "mores."

The right to sue is a given but lawyers must, if they have any decency, be principled. Maybe just chastising them in the media would improve their demeanor, although money makes whores out of at lot of people. We could just call this the John Edward's effect. I believe that creating conflict through hate speech should be punished in some way. The Al Sharpton effect. Being chastised in the media might be enough to stop people stirring up conflict between the races or different groups.

I now believe that abortion is not the answer, although there are some circumstances where it should be available as a medical procedure. Rape victims and when a mother's health is in jeopardy are examples. Partial birth abortion is equivalent to murder but we must govern with the laws of the United States and right now abortion is legal.

First Saturday Of Each Month

We must end the race problem. A good start would be for the media and politicians to ignore race as a subject. An example of not ignoring race was the replacement for Barack Obama's Senate seat. The argument that this Senate seat was held by a black person and should remain that way, is an argument that should lose every time. All sports select their players based on ability, not the color of their skin. This is how all other positions should be filled. Politicians and the media keep this issue stirred up making the public constantly aware of something that should not even be considered. The media is obsessed with what nationality, race, ethnic background, sex, sexual orientation, a person is, it is ridiculous. Diversification of appointees is possible without fanfare.

The homeless problem could be solve with a liberal idea. That would be the WPA, (works, progress, administration). Maybe, just maybe, Roosevelt had an idea. Gather up all the homeless and give them room and board at the various military bases. Give them classes on hygiene, civic pride, simple job skills, etc. Pay each person $20.00 per day. Give them $5.00 in their pocket and start a bank account with the remainder. Stipulate that they may leave anytime after 100 days. They will then have $1500 in the bank to get a room, a few clothes and a paying job. There could be some help with job placement if needed. People must be responsible in this society. The present homeless approach, which makes certain people feel good, is to feed them in soup kitchens, and offer shelters. This merely helps them to be homeless. A Chinese proverb: "Give a man a fish and you feed him for a day. Teach a man to fish and you feed him for a lifetime." Can we never learn from history?

Gangs, another big problem, with no government solution, surprise, surprise when did it have a solution for anything. The gang problem will decrease when the drug solution I recommended is implemented. It could also be partially solved using the same technique as my homeless solution, except it would need a very strict disciplinary program. A gang in the neighborhood could be a good thing if they did community work, but first we need to break their criminal patterns. Removing drugs from the scene will be a start.

First Saturday Of Each Month

Notes on This Chapter

Chapter Nineteen

A short civic lesson on how this government functions.

The first thing to understand is that the power of the United States government is in the hands of the people. The people should be motivated to learn and understand how the government works, then they can take advantage of the people's power. Do not vote for someone just because they had more money to spend on campaigning. Vote for them because of their beliefs and stated policies. Do not vote for them because of their party affiliation, vote for them because of how they will use the constitution to solve problems.

"Change," was the main campaign theme for the last election yet many of the same people are still in the congress and the senate. What kind of change is this and what does it all mean? We changed the President with white hair to one with black hair, temporarily. We changed from Republican to Democrat. What we needed to change was our approach to solving the problems, they certainly are not going to be solved by just throwing money at them. We the people, must demand, that before the election, candidates inform us on how they intend to solve the various problems. In the last election, not one person that I know of who was running for office, informed us of how they intended to solve the various problems.

It is necessary to understand that the President does not have the

Power to Declare War. It seems that President Bush is the one who receives all the blame for the war in Iraq. However, Congress is the one responsible for the Declaration of War and at the time Congress had a Democratic majority. The president can create a police action, but this is not what happened in Iraq. The President is the commander in Chief of the Military, but he carries out congressional orders.

President Bush deserves credit for protecting us from terrorism after 9/11, but he has not protected us from illegal border crossings. The latter is just as big a threat to our way of life as terrorism. Also at the time he left office, President Bush was losing the so called war on drugs.

Congress makes all laws, not the judicial branch of the government, it is the judicial branch of governments purpose to enforce the laws made by congress, yes they can overturn a law if it is counter to the constitution.

Congress has not protected us from financial disasters, has not even tried to solve the social security problem, has muddled in the education system to where it's an ongoing disaster and has done very little to help with the energy crisis. Congresses progress on problems appears to be nonexistent.

We the people must get involved, through the voting booth, pen and paper, which would include e-mail, phone, community meetings, etc. Lets make it happen now.

The President appoints all judicial members of the government, but congress must approve of these appointments. This approval must be based on the person's ability and desire to uphold the constitution of the United States. In the past many appointments have been made on a person's ideological thoughts and deeds, the people must show their displeasure at this type of appointment.

The United States is a participative democracy, which means the people have a duty to participate in electing our government. For this to be successful, the people must be informed and educated about how the process works and then be able to determine if a particular candidate for the office is qualified. This can only be accomplished through education. Students should be taught how to make a difference in their communities through getting involved in community projects, going to council meetings, etc. To receive U.S. Citizenship immigrants should be required to speak and understand English, have some knowledge of how the United States government works and why we pledge allegiance to the flag. We must make this a full participative democracy again with people who are informed and knowledgeable of our place in history. Maybe some sort of civic pride type of projects in the communities. Get local adults with their children involved, by participating in government functions. We must bring back community pride, with local neighborhood projects. This country can again be the greatest on earth, with hope, change for the good and full participation democracy.

Many politicians love "voter dependency." That way they obtain reelection based on promises not performance. We do not want that type of politician, we want the type that will solve problems and create a better way of life.

Back to civics, congress is the governing body that spends the tax dollars. The President submits a budget, but it needs congressional approval and it is congress that spends the money. We the people must encourage these congress Men and Women to spend it wisely.

The electoral college's function is to elect the President of the United States. It was created within the Constitution. The constitution is a big part of civics. It is in Chapter sixteen, go back, read it again, study it, it is our road map.

It is important to study and understand American History, if we are going to participate in this democracy. Take a history class at your local college or night school at your local high school. Make history fun for your family and friends. We should learn a lot from history but the opposite seems to be true. The repeating of mistakes is a very big waste of money and time.

First Saturday Of Each Month

Notes on Civics

Chapter Twenty

What is wrong with America?

Picture a road going on to infinity, with Republicans on one side and Democrats on the other, as far as you can see. They all have leaf blowers and are blowing the dirt towards the opposite side.

The caption reads:
"Bipartisanship"

Definitions of political alignments

There are two political parties within which we can work to save this country. All other ways, third parties for example are ineffective and a waste of resources. Canada and New Zealand are examples with their minor parties and minority governments which create huge pork spending just to make a coalition. The Republican party, in my opinion, appears to have the best ability to solve the problems. The Democratic party is too negative on all issues, they do not discuss solutions or ideas. Their attitude is "they could do it better" and "the Republicans did it wrong." We do need discussions on ideas and ideas from all sources would be welcome. There are several very good fiscal conservatives in the Democratic Party and they should be reelected. There are fiscal irresponsible members of the Republican Party and they should be voted out of office.

For a perspective of the two parties, read their platforms: www.gop. com Republican platform. www.dem.com Democratic platform. See Chapter Twenty-two to get some feel for the two platforms.

What we do not need are the moderates and the mavericks. It is not helpful to any cause to have people compromising there principles just because there are differing points of view. Meeting the opposition half way to form a compromise does not solve anything. There is usually more than one way to solve a problem but to compromise ideas from a hundred legislators is not the solution.

With an informed public, primaries could be used to separate the candidates with good conservative ideas from the ones with compromise in mind. The people and grass root organizations must use letters, emails and the telephone to keep their representatives acting responsibly. It boils down to a well informed public would be able to get the government to solve the problems.

They would also be able to stop power abuses, the quote: "Power tends to corrupt, and absolute power corrupts absolutely" is very, very true. The well entrenched legislators who are in "safe seats" are much of the problem with the government and its power structure. The government runs on a seniority system, which means that the people in "safe seats" move to positions of power, not because of their expertise, but solely on time in office. In this last election the congress had a single digit approval rating yet roughly a 95% of congress was reelected. This points to a problem that must be addressed. There seems to be an unwritten rule that if an incumbent is running for a seat, all other possible candidates disappear. Term limits would be a way of solving this but then we will throw out the wheat with the chaff. However, this may be the best solution.

Legislators have control of Federal money that has come from the taxpayers. They are able to use this money for "Pork barrel spending," often just to enable them to become reelected. Each item requiring money should be judged on its own merit not added to other unrelated legislation. I read somewhere: 'Man does not know everything but when he acts as though he does, disaster follows.' Substitute "Legislator" for "Man" and that appears to be what is happening in Congress. I have never heard a legislator admit to not knowing something, therefore disasters happen on a regular basis. The financial crisis is the last example at this writing. The two entrenched legislators most responsible for overviewing the financial institutions, have, in my mind, very little knowledge of how it all works. Somehow they gave the impression that they did and rejected most, if not all, of the outside help offered. In some cases this was potential problem solving legislation.

Republicans and Democrats are made up of the following categories. Fiscal conservatives, found mostly in the Republican party. These should be the people running the government. Social conservatives should be in think tanks, coming up with solutions to make the world a better place. Liberal thinkers, found mostly in the Democratic party, should also be in think tanks helping with world problems. Moderates in both parties should rethink their positions and jump into one of the previous groups. Mavericks should change careers and join the media. Far right thinkers, perhaps ones who think Religious orders should be running the government, should be in editorial positions of failing newspapers. Far left thinkers, perhaps ones who think that the labor unions should be running the government, should join the far righters and start their own newspaper. Most of the above groups are the ones causing the problems with our government. The federal government should be making very few social rules. Social engineering must stop. The government must not be allowed to force lending institutions to make loan's to people who have no ability to repay them, just because "it feels good" for everyone to own their own home.

In conclusion the voting public needs to be informed and vote the people into office who will do the right thing.

Notes on the Political Parties

Chapter Twenty-one

List of conservative web sites and other reading material

www.heritage.org ——————-
This must be everyday reading for people who care.

www.gop.com
www.dem.com
Other related sites for the Heritage Foundation.
33 Minutes
www.familyfacts.org
The Founders' Almanac
www.insideronline.org
Iran Briefing Room
Iraq Progress
The Margaret Thatcher Center for Freedom
www.myheritage.org
www.nationalsecurity.org
www.overcriminalized.com
Policy Experts
www.reagansheritage.org

www.thomas.loc.gov.com
You must read this web site, you will find out what your representatives are doing.

www.unionreports.gov
You must read this site to find out what your unions are spending your money on.

Books:

How To Change The World by David Bornstein
Comment: Another good view on change.

The Conservative Mind by Russell Kirk
Comment: One of the few people that can express an understanding of Conservatism.

The Triumph of the Airheads and the retreat from Commonsense by Shelley Gare
Comment: This is about Australian Politics but it does hit home about the people in charge.

Term Limits, written by Vince Flynn
Comment: This is not how we should term limit our Representatives but it does touch on why.

Air Con by Ian Wishart
Comment: This is about a seriously inconvenient truth about Global Warming.

Political Animals by Jane Clifton
Comment: Written about New Zealand politicians but it does explain the type of personalities and ego's that we are dealing with.

Notes on other Books to read

Chapter Twenty-two

What is wrong with America?"

Picture: A Politician handing out approval slips for medical procedures and other health care problems.

The Caption reads:
"It will never work and has never worked"

Liberal ideas that have not worked in the past nor will they in the future. Also a look at the two political parties platforms, with comments.

Building the economy from the bottom up. It has been tried in Zimbabwe, taking the land from the rich and giving it to the poor. Their economy is probably the worst in the world whereas formerly they were feeding themselves and other parts of the world.

The pilgrims, when they immigrated to the new world, began by pooling their produce. Whoever needed something just went there and took it. Guess how well this worked? Some people did not contribute but just took what they needed.

Universal Health Care is a "feel good" liberal idea. It does not work where it is being used and it will not work in America. There are two reasons that make it work at all.

The first is that many patients recover without a doctors care. Socialized medicine creates limited access to specialists so many times a patient is better (or worse, dead) and no longer needs a doctor by the time his name is called. The really bad consequences of universal health care are, that knowing the difficulties of obtaining an appointment, the patient does not try to see a doctor until his situation is critical.

The second reason it works at all is because you can have private health insurance, or just pay for services rendered. Without these two things universal health care would be a total flop. Socialized medicine has been established in the UK for more than 50 years yet if you need a hip replacement you could be on a waiting list for 2 years. Even chemotherapy often requires a 6 month wait. Canada, also uses this system and something that might be diagnosed using an MRI may not even be available.

One of the better plans, in the Democratic platform, is that all families have the same health insurance coverage that congress enjoys. If this is accomplished, without bankrupting the United States government, I will be the first to congratulate the framers of this legislation.

The minimum wage was established to improve the lifestyle of the working person. If this worked increasing it drastically could really improve the working persons lifestyle. However, once the minimum wage is increased, all other workers need a raise too. This just causes inflation. Employers, who are now paying more for labor, raise their prices to compensate. The workers then need more money, it never ends. There should be some sort of base, but do not treat minimum wage as how a person earns a living. When a person develops job skills, he goes beyond minimum wage. There should be a lower wage for young and unskilled people to enter the work place so that companies and businesses can afford to offer training.

From the Democratic Platform:

We come together at a defining moment in the history of our nation – the nation that led the Twentieth century, built a thriving middle class, defeated fascism and communism, and provided bountiful opportunity to many. We Democrats have a special commitment to this promise of America. We believe that every American, whatever their background or station in life, should have the chance to get a good education, to work at a good job with good wages, to raise and provide for a family, to live in safe surroundings, and to retire with dignity and security. We believe that quality and affordable health care is a basic right. We believe that each succeeding generation should have the opportunity, through hard work, service, and sacrifice, to enjoy a brighter future than the last.

Today, we are at a crossroads. As we meet, we are in the sixth year of a two-front war. Our economy is struggling. Our planet is in peril.

A great nation now demands that its leaders abandon the politics of partisan division and find creative solutions to promote the common good. A people that prizes candor, accountability, and fairness insists that a government of the people must level with them and champion the interests of all American families. A land of historic resourcefulness has lost its patience with elected officials who have failed to lead. It is time for a change. We can do better.

And so, Democrats — through the most open platform process in history — are reaching out today to Republicans, Independents, and all Americans who hunger for a new direction a reason to hope. Today, at a defining moment in our history, the Democratic Party resolves to renew America's promise.

Over the past eight years, our nation's leaders have failed us. Sometimes they invited calamity, rushing us into an ill-considered war in Iraq. But other times, when calamity arrived in the form of hurricanes or financial storms, they sat back, doing too little too late, and too poorly. The list of failures of this Administration is historic.

The American Dream is at risk. Incomes are down and foreclosures are up. Millions of our fellow citizens have no health insurance while families working longer hours are pressed for time to care for their children and aging parents. Gas and home heating costs are squeezing seniors and working families alike. We are less secure and less respected in the world. After September 11, we could have built the foundation for a new American century, but instead we instigated an unnecessary war in Iraq before finishing a necessary war in Afghanistan. Careless policies, inept stewardship and the broken politics of this Administration have taken their toll on our economy, our security and our reputation.

But even worse than the conditions we find ourselves in are the false promises that brought us here. The Republican leadership said they would keep us safe, but they overextended our military and failed to respond to new challenges. They said they would be compassionate conservatives, but they failed to rescue our citizens from the rooftops of New Orleans, neglected our veterans, and denied health insurance to children. They promised fiscal responsibility but instead gave tax cuts to the wealthy few and squandered almost a trillion dollars in Iraq. They promised reform but allowed the oil companies to write our energy agenda and the credit card companies to write the bankruptcy rules.

These are not just policy failures. They are failures of a broken politics –a politics that rewards self-interest over the common interest and the short-term over the long-term, that puts our government at the service of the powerful. A politics that creates a state-of-the-art system for doling out favors and shuts out the voice of the American people.

So, we come together not only to replace this President and his party –and not only to offer policies that will undo the damage they have wrought. Today, we pledge a return to core moral principles like stewardship, service to others, personal responsibility, shared sacrifice and a fair shot for all –values that emanate from the integrity and optimism of our Founders and generations of Americans since. Today, we Democrats offer leaders –from the White House to the State House – worthy of this country's trust.

We will start by renewing the American Dream for a new era – with the same new hope and new ideas that propelled Franklin Delano Roosevelt towards the New Deal and John F. Kennedy to the New Frontier. We will provide immediate relief to working people who have lost their jobs, families who are in danger of losing their homes, and those who—no matter how hard they work—are seeing prices go up more than their income.

First Saturday Of Each Month

My Comments:

You may read this several times and say, "Yes! But what solutions have they really promised that will change anything. Absolutely nothing. What they said is: "they can do it better," yeah right! They also said: "the American dream is dead," it certainly will be when they finish what they have now started.

More Democratic Platform:

Jumpstart the Economy and Provide Middle Class Americans Immediate Relief

We will provide an immediate energy rebate to American families struggling with the record price of gasoline and the skyrocketing cost of other necessities – to spend on those basic needs and energy efficient measures. We will devote $50 billion to jumpstarting the economy, helping economic growth, and preventing another one million jobs from being lost. This will include assistance to states and localities to prevent them from having to cut their vital services like education, health care, and infrastructure. We will quickly implement the housing bill recently passed by Congress and ensure that states and localities that have been hard-hit by the housing crisis can avoid cuts in vital services. We support investments in infrastructure to replenish the highway trust fund, invest in road and bridge maintenance and fund new, fast-tracked projects to repair schools. We believe that it is essential to take immediate steps to stem the loss of manufacturing jobs. Taking these immediate measures will provide good jobs and will help the economy today. But generating truly shared prosperity is only possible if we also address our most significant long-run challenges like the rising cost of health care, energy, and education.

My Comments:

More generalized solutions for perceived problems. They are going to stem the loss of manufacturing jobs, just how are they going to do that without creating havoc in the international community.

They have just created more questions WHAT? HOW? WHEN? With WHO'S money?

Just for variety some from the Republican Platform:

This is a platform of enduring principle, not passing convenience -the product of the most open and transparent process in American political history. We offer it to our fellow Americans in the assurance that our Republican ideals are those that unify our country: Courage in the face of foreign foes. An optimistic patriotism, driven by a passion for freedom. Devotion to the inherent dignity and rights of every person. Faith in the virtues of self-reliance, civic commitment, and concern for one another. Distrust of government's interference in people's lives. Dedication to a rule of law that both protects and preserves liberty. We present this platform at an uncertain point in time. Our country remains at war and committed to victory, but reckless political forces would imperil that goal and endanger our nation. In the economy and in society at large, it is a time of transformation. But the American people will meet these challenges. Even with its uncertainties, they embrace the future, but they are also too wise to rush headlong into it. We are an adventurous, risk-taking people, but we are not gamblers. A sound democracy trusts new leadership but insists that it demonstrate the old virtues: the character and the command that, in times of conflict and crisis, have led the Republic through its trials.

This platform likewise rests on proven truths and tested wisdom as it looks ahead, both to deal with present challenges and to explore possibilities that may sometimes seem beyond our grasp. It shows what the American people can accomplish when government respects their rights, conserves their resources, and calls upon their love of country. It is not a tribute to bigger government. Our platform is presented with enthusiasm and confidence in a vision for the future, but also with genuine humility, humility before God and before a nation of free and independent thinkers. As the party of ideas, rather than a mere coalition of interests, we consider vigorous debate a strength, not a weakness. Indeed, we are a party - as we are a nation - of mavericks. Yet we stand united today because we are the one party that speaks to all Americans - conservatives, moderates, libertarians, independents, and even liberals. We welcome all to our deliberations in the firm belief that the principles embodied in this platform will prove to be as compelling and persuasive as they are vital and enduring. We do not fear disagreement, and we do not demand conformity, but we do fight for our principles with confidence that the best ideas will prevail in the end.

My Comments:

Just like the beginning of the Democratic Platform, you may read this several times and say, "Yes! Its great," which it is, but again there are no real solutions.

Republican Tax Policy: Protecting Hardworking Americans

The most important distinction between Republicans and the leadership of today's Democratic Party concerning taxes is not just that we believe you should keep more of what you earn. That's true, but there is a more fundamental distinction. It concerns the purpose of taxation. We believe government should tax only to raise money for its essential functions. Today's Democratic Party views the tax code as a tool for social engineering. They use it to control our behavior, steer our choices, and change the way we live our lives. The Republican Party will put a stop to both social engineering and corporate handouts by simplifying tax policy, eliminating special deals, and putting those saved dollars back into the taxpayers' pockets.

The Republican Agenda: Using Tax Relief to Grow the Economy

Sound tax policy alone may not ensure economic success, but terrible tax policy does guarantee economic failure. Along with making the 2001 and 2003 tax cuts permanent so American families will not face a large tax hike, Republicans will advance tax policies to support American families, promote savings and innovation, and put us on a path to fundamental tax reform.

Lower Taxes on Families and Individuals

American families with children are the hardest hit during any economic downturn. Republicans will lower their tax burden by doubling the exemption for dependents.

New technology should not occasion more taxation. We will permanently ban internet access taxes and stop all new cell phone taxes. For the sake of family farms and small businesses, we will continue our fight against the federal death tax. The Alternative Minimum Tax, a stealth levy on the middle-class that unduly targets large families, must be repealed. Republicans support tax credits for health care and medical expenses.

Keeping Good Jobs in America

America's producers can compete successfully in the international arena ó as long as they have a level playing field. Today's tax code is tilted against them, with one of the highest corporate tax rates of all developed countries. That not only hurts American investors, managers, and the U.S. balance of trade; it also sends American jobs overseas. We support a major reduction in the corporate tax rate so that American companies stay competitive with their foreign counterparts and American jobs can remain in this country.

Promoting Savings through the Tax Code

We support a tax code that encourages personal savings. High tax rates discourage thrift by penalizing the return on savings and should be replaced with incentives to save. We support a plan to encourage employers to offer automatic enrollment in tax-deferred savings programs. The current limits on tax-free savings accounts should be removed.

Fundamental Tax Reform

Over the long run, the mammoth IRS tax code must be replaced with a system that is simple, transparent, and fair while maximizing economic growth and job creation. As a transition, we support giving all taxpayers the option of filing under current rules or under a two-rate flat tax with generous deductions for families. This gradual approach is the taxpayers' best hope of overcoming the lobbyist legions that have thwarted past simplification efforts. As a matter of principle, we oppose retroactive taxation, and we condemn attempts by judges, at any level of government, to seize the power of the purse by ordering higher taxes. Because of the vital role of religious organizations, charities and fraternal benevolent societies in fostering charity and patriotism, they should not be subject to taxation. In any fundamental restructuring of federal taxation, to guard against the possibility of hyper-taxation of the American people, any value added tax or national sales tax must be tied to simultaneous repeal of the Sixteenth Amendment, which established the federal income tax.

The Democrats Plan to Raise Your Taxes

The last thing Americans need right now is tax hikes. On the federal level, Republicans lowered taxes in 2001 and 2003 in order to encourage economic growth, put more money in the pockets of every taxpayer, and make the system fairer. It worked. If Congress had then controlled its spending, we could have done even more. Ever since those tax cuts were enacted, the Democratic Party has been clear about its goals: It wants to raise taxes by eliminating those Republican tax reductions. The impact on American families would be disastrous: Marginal tax rates would rise. This is in addition to their proposal to target millions of taxpayers with even higher rates. The "marriage penalty" would return for two-earner couples. The child tax credit would fall to half its current value. Small businesses would lose their tax relief. The federal death tax would be enormously increased. Investment income - the seed money for new jobs ó would be eaten away by higher rates for dividend and capital gain income. All that and more would amount to an annual tax hike upwards of $250 billion ó almost $700 per taxpayer every year, for a total of $1.1 trillion in additional taxes over the next decade. That is what today's Democratic Party calls "tax fairness." We call it an unconscionable assault on the paychecks and pocketbooks of every hardworking American household. Their promises to aim their tax hikes at families with high incomes is a smokescreen; history shows that when Democrats want more money, they raise taxes on everyone.

My Comments:

The one thing that the Republican party gets right is that taxes need to be low. Just cutting them is not enough, a complete overhaul is required. See my chapter on Tax Reform Chapter Four.

Back to the Democratic Platform:

Affordable, Quality Health Care Coverage for All Americans. If one thing came through in the platform hearings, it was that Democrats are united around a commitment that every American man, woman, and child be guaranteed affordable, comprehensive healthcare. In meeting after meeting, people expressed moral outrage with a health care crisis that leaves millions of Americans–including nine million children–without health insurance and millions more struggling to pay rising costs for poor quality care. Half of all personal bankruptcies in America are caused by medical bills. We spend more on health care than any other country, but we're ranked 47th in life expectancy and 43rd in child mortality. Our nation faces epidemics of obesity and chronic diseases as well as new threats like pandemic flu and bioterrorism. Yet despite all of this, less than four cents of every health care dollar is spent on prevention and public health.

The American people understand that good health is the foundation of individual achievement and economic prosperity. Ensuring quality, affordable health care for every single American is essential to children's education, workers' productivity and businesses' competitiveness. We believe that covering all is not just a moral imperative, but is necessary to making our health system workable and affordable. Doing so would end cost-shifting from the uninsured, promote prevention and wellness, stop insurance discrimination, help eliminate health care disparities, and achieve savings through competition, choice, innovation, and higher quality care. While there are different approaches within the Democratic Party about how best to achieve the commitment of covering every American, with everyone in and no one left out, we stand united to achieve this fundamental objective through the legislative process.

We therefore oppose those who advocate policies that would thrust millions of Americans out of their current private employer-based coverage without providing them access to an affordable, comprehensive alternative, thereby subjecting them to the kind of insurance discrimination that leads to excessive premiums or coverage denials for older and sicker Americans. We reject those who have steadfastly opposed insurance coverage expansions for millions of our nation's children while they have protected overpayments to insurers and allowed underpayments to our nation's doctors. Our vision of a strengthened and improved health care system for all Americans stands in stark contrast to the Republican Party's.

My Comment:

This is only a small sample of the Democratic Health care plan from their platform. Read it in it's entirety on their web site, www.dem.com. It all sounds great but they miss the important parts. A person should be able to shop for the best care at an acceptable price. The FDA needs to be changed so that innovative procedures and medicines can be introduced without requiring millions and millions of dollars being needed to obtain approval. Government cannot just mandate health care and it will happen. They need to remove the barriers that exist, so that private industry can solve the problems. They do have something right in this, prevention is one of the keys to improving health care.

More Democratic Platform:

Good Jobs with Good Pay

In the platform hearings, Americans expressed dismay that people who are willing to study and work cannot get a job that pays enough to live on in the current economy. Democrats are committed to an economic policy that produces good jobs with good pay and benefits. That is why we support the right to organize. We know that when unions are allowed to do their job of making sure that workers get their fair share, they pull people out of poverty and create a stronger middle class. We will strengthen the ability of workers to organize unions and fight to pass the Employee Free Choice Act. We will restore pro-worker voices to the National Labor Relations Board and the National Mediation Board and we support overturning the NLRB's and NMB's many harmful decisions that undermine the collective bargaining rights of millions of workers. We will ensure that federal employees, including public safety officers who put their lives on the line every day, have the right to bargain collectively, and we will fix the broken bargaining process at the Federal Aviation Administration. We will fight to ban the permanent replacement of striking workers, so that workers can stand up for themselves without worrying about losing their livelihoods. We will continue to vigorously oppose "Right-to-Work" Laws and "paycheck protection" efforts whenever they are proposed. Suspending labor protections during national emergencies compounds the devastation from the emergency. We opposed suspension of Davis-Bacon following Hurricane Katrina, and we support broad application of Davis-Bacon worker protections to all federal projects. We will stop the abuse of privatization of government jobs. We will end the exploitative practice of employers wrongly misclassifying workers as independent contractors.

My Comment:

Now this is scary stuff, why would they promise this, the answer is the unions of today have too much power. The unions, like government, are promoting things that make the workers dependent on them. It should be the other way around, the government and unions should be dependent on the workers.

These quotes from the two different platforms show equal rhetoric. Neither party shows any clear cut solutions or even suggested solutions. Yes, we want change but not just verbal change, we want solutions to problems. NOW!

My Platform if I were to compete with these two parties would be:

I will end all poverty in the world. I will also stop all wars and create peace in the world. Health care will be provided for every person. Everyone will have a right to a well paid job. Crime will be eliminated. The war on drugs will be won. I will end all racial and sexual discrimination. My government will provide for you if you are not able to provide for yourself. Maybe I will even try to stop all natural disasters.

My Comment:

If you think this is rhetoric, reread both parties platforms again. You will see that change is not going to happen unless we make it happen. Get on board and let's do it. The first Saturday of each month will be the key to getting there attention.

Notes on the Political Platforms

Chapter Twenty-three

What is wrong with America?

Picture: A student, wearing a dunce's cap on his little head, sitting in the corner.

The Caption reads:
"If the present is any indication, this is a future politician."

List of Names

If the following list of names makes your eyes tear up, or brings bile to your throat, you are a Conservative. Maybe it just makes you wonder how these people advanced to their present positions. They did it mostly through the electoral process, scary. One person, not yet on the list, is Barack Obama. My real hope is that he will do the right thing.

1) Nancy Pelosi
2) Harry Reid
3) Ted Kennedy
4) Chris Dodd
5) Barney Frank
6) John Conyers
7) Hillary Clinton
8) Bill Clinton
9) Bill Richardson
10) Janet Napolitano
11) Dick Durbin
12) Diane Feinstein
13) Barbara Boxer

14) Jimmy Carter

15) Albert Gore

16) Jesse Jackson

17) Al Frankin

18) Al Sharpton

19) Janet Reno

20) Madeline Albright

21) Bill Ayers

22) Rod Blagojevick

23) Michael Moore

24) George Soros

Add your favorite names to this list

Chapter Twenty-four

What is wrong with America?

Picture: Mobs of people talking on cell phones walking towards a cliff edge. The front ones are falling off.

The Caption reads:
"People calling Obama wondering how he can help them."

What is wrong with America?

Picture: The President, with a white beard dressed in a red suit. He's passing out something for everyone from an acorn bag.

The Caption reads:
"Obama's unlimited stimulus package"

Obama

Obama had been in office about 50 days when I started this Chapter. I am still giving him the benefit of the doubt, but my patience is wearing thin. He is throwing money at most of the problems, which will not, in itself, solve any problems. If money solved problems the USA would not have any problems. He has appointed ex government employees to most of his appointed positions, this is not change, this is politics at its worst. Recommendations are being made that the government become partners in private industry, for example banks and the auto industry. This scares the hell out of me, Socialism comes to mind and that is not an option.

He is closing terrorist jail facilities. May I assume we are not going to take any more prisoners, which is not a bad idea!

He has stopped some free trade agreement talks with some of the better countries. What kind of message does this send to the world?

Embryo stem cell research is the latest government intrusion into social engineering. Yes, we need stem cell research and it needs some government funding. However, Obama is putting Congress in charge of policing this research, my immediate thought is, who was in charge of policing the financial industry? Talk about a nightmare?

See Chapter Twenty-three for a list of potential leaders in this policing.

Whose ideas are on the TelePrompTers? It is to be hoped that they are Obama's, if not, we are all in bigger trouble.

Obama's Stimulus Packages:

When all the Republican members of congress vote against it, it means one of two things: The Republicans are just making a statement or haven't a clue how important it is to stimulate the economy. The alternate is that there is things wrong with this stimulus package, and it should not be passed in it's present state. I presume it will pass. If it fixes the problems the Democrats win and the Republicans lose. If it does not fix the problem, we all lose. The results will probably be inconclusive. Some things in the package may help and others will just add to the overall general mess.

It is to be hoped that we are still carrying a big stick with all the soft talk about Iran.

I am not sure that I want a television star for a President, but this seems to be the case right now.

My patience has run out. The new budget has been proposed at $3,700,000,000,000.00, which I find totally unacceptable. This, after Trillion dollar bailouts, yes, plural. Now I think I heard the Trillion word again in the G20 summit. We are putting the future in jeopardy, which is not fair to the coming generations of illegal Immigrants. Just kidding about the immigrants but it is certainly unfair to our children's children. Obama, you in my opinion, are now on the list in the previous chapter. We must implement my proposed solutions and end this nonsense.

A news item on the internet May 24, 2009

> ISLAMABAD – The Taliban left so many mutilated bodies at the crossing — some hanging from trees with threatening

notes — that Pakistanis in the Swat Valley's main town took to calling it "bloody intersection."

My comments:

To think we are discussing the water boarding of three military combatants, like it is a major human rights disaster!

We now have a supreme court nominee that has a warm and fuzzy feeling about law and the constitution. Great!

North Korea tested a large atomic bomb and our Presidents comment is: "He is disappointed with them for not abiding by the UN rules." Yeah Right, like they give a s—

The latest! A two thousand page proposed health care plan. We need less government pages of rules not more. What we need to do is repair the present system as suggested in Chapter Seven.

Notes on Obama

Chapter Twenty-five

What is wrong with America?

Picture: Money by the basket load, being used to create all the rhetoric on television, which goes on for ever.

The Caption reads:
"Campaigning! Make it simple, stop the rhetoric"

First Saturday Of Each Month

Money in politics

The first thing that needs to be addressed is the time that politicians campaign for office. It is unbelievable that campaigns can last for up to two years. Around three months should be long enough to promote their ideas to the public. Smear tactics used in campaigning, should be left to the investigative media. The people running for office should use their capital for informing the public on how they are going to solve the problems. A war of ideas is what the voting public should have to separate, then they can vote responsibly.

All campaign donations should be reported on a daily basis in some form of structured format that the investigative media can analyze. The public should also have access to this information. It should be as simple as:

John Doe, Forest, Ca.-$3.00

Sam Smith, Little Rock, AK-$10,000

Joe Sixpack, Backyard Barbecue, MI-$200,000

I'm A. Nut, High School Days, NE-$29.95

China Mafia, Mainland China $700,000,000,000,000

All anonymous donations, coming into a campaign headquarters should be divided equally between all parties running for that office. The same thing should be applied at party headquarters. If it's anonymous then it must be shared with the other viable parties. Public money collected from tax returns, (hopefully that dreaded form will be gone), should be divided based on voting registration percentages.

Print media, when you endorse a candidate, it would be helpful if you would list your detailed reasons for this endorsement. "He is for change," or "he is a very likable person," or "the women like his personality," are not reasons. The reasons would be "his policies" and "how he is going to solve the problems."

Notes on Money in Politics

Chapter Twenty-six

What will help make things right with America?

Picture: Family and friends discussing politics.

The Caption reads:
"Never discuss politics or religion?"
"What idiot made that rule?"

Educational Ideas spreading the word

Martin Luther King, Jr., stood at the Lincoln Memorial, and among other things he spoke these words: "We have come to this hallowed ground to remind Americans of the fierce urgency of now. This is no time to relax in the luxury of cooling off or to take the tranquilizing drug of gradualism."

- We must heed this call for urgency and solve these problems now. Movie theaters have pre-show quiz questions Perhaps they could be used to attract peoples attention.

- Ads and comments in local throwaway papers.

- How about a TV game show?

- Local gatherings with speakers and/or just to express ideas.

- Conservative organizations could justify spending money to give away free items similar to incentives offered by Time Share sales offices to encourage people to listen to their advantages. We must engage the public.

- Free concerts with opening lectures on conservatism.

- Start discussion groups in all kinds of settings, schools, retirement communities, neighborhoods, etc.

- E-mail passages from this book to everybody on your list, get them talking about the problems and then the solutions. If you agree with some of the solutions, send them to your Representative in Washington.

- Ads on yahoo and other e-mail servers could have contests for the best ideas to solve problems.

- The absolute best way to spread the word that the people want to be in charge will be to have monthly rallies at the various state capitals and in Washington, D.C. Make it the first Saturday of each month and bring a copy of this book, with your notes and suggestions, to discuss with other rally attendees. Peaceful and litter free rallies are a necessity!

Recommended signs:

FIX THE USA

FIX THE USA's TAX SYSTEM

FIX SOCIAL SECURITY

FIX THE UNITED NATIONS OR GET OUT

FIX HEALTH CARE

FIX THE EDUCATIONAL SYSTEM

FIX THE DRUG PROBLEM

FIX IMMIGRATION

FIX THE ENERGY CRISIS

FIX THE FINANCIAL CRISIS

First Saturday Of Each Month

FIX THE HOMELESS PROBLEM

FIX THE GANG CULTURE PROBLEM

FIX WELFARE

STOP THE RHETORIC AND FIX THE PROBLEMS WE WANT CHANGE, FIX THE PROBLEMS

GOVERNMENT MEMBERS IF YOU DO NOT HAVE A SOLUTION RESIGN

You will make your own signs also. We need to do this every first Saturday of the month until the problems are solved. In between, we e-mail, call, or write our representatives to find out why they have not been working on, or fixing these problems. We can win this battle.

Your ideas for signs

Chapter Twenty-seven

What could be right with America?

Picture: Yourself getting involved with electing your next representative.

The Caption reads:
"Look out politicians here we come"

How to get involved in various ways

Now is the key, it will be too late unless we do it now.Start or join a conservative club in your school, neighborhood or community.

- Teach your children, grandchildren about conservative principles.

- Volunteer for candidates of your choice, during election times.

- Run for local elections.

- Send money to your preferred candidates.

- Talk to your neighbors about politics and conservative ideas.

- Write your local paper on topics you are passionate about.

- Call your Representatives on various legislation.

- E-mail your Representatives on a regular basis about your concerns and thoughts.

- Vote, and volunteer at voting locations, also help with "get out the vote programs."

- Volunteer at Churches and local charities, but make

sure they know you are conservative and this is what we do to help people.

- Listen to conservative talk radio, frequent their sponsors.
- Read books on the various political subjects.
- Go to community government meetings and make your voice heard, in an intelligent way.
- Support your local police and sheriffs.
- Volunteer at local schools to help monitor playground, etc.
- Organize community projects to improve life in the community.
- Take classes at local high schools or colleges in Civics and American History.
- Read such things as the 2008 Party platforms and discuss these with friends, neighbors and the community at large. We must get involved with our government. Vote for the people who will make a difference, understand how it works and give views for solutions.
- To re-enforce my previously stated idea: The absolute best way to spread the word that the people want to be in charge will be to have monthly rallies at the various state capitals and in Washington, D.C. Make it the first Saturday of each month and bring a copy of this book, with your notes and suggestions, to discuss with other rally attendees. Peaceful and litter free rallies are a necessity!
- Start a "How to save the USA" club.

How I am going to get Involved

Chapter Twenty-eight

What will be right with America?

Picture: A million man, woman and child march in the US capital on the first Saturday of each month. They are carrying signs that tell the legislators what needs to be fixed. I can see the headlines in the newspapers and the lead stories on television very vividly.

The Caption is:
"Let me be a part of this fantastic revolution."

Overall Thoughts

If you only take one idea from this book, make it that the people of the US are the leaders of the country and should study and work harder in that role. In voting for a candidate it's necessary to know what he/she stands for and how problems will be solved. Keep in touch with them and know how they are performing. Let them know, on a regular basis, how they should be governing.

The next idea to take from this book is that it's necessary to get involved by choosing a problem and working towards it's solution.

Young people your problem should be a solution for social security. Let's be heard and get this done.

We must have a discussion about ideas on how to solve problems. We cannot allow our leaders to just talk change. We need specifics on their approach to a solution, not just rhetoric. Once a solution has been agreed upon we must all work towards it's success.

One continuous problem is the growth of government. We must pass laws that limit the size and power of government. We, the people, must keep the pressure on our representatives to do our bidding. This will also expand the choices that are available to individuals.

Let us get out there and do our part, however small it might be.

Yes, we can make a difference, we just have to do it. See item twenty of chapter twenty-seven, we all can do this and it will make a difference. We are going to win this battle to save the USA.

Doctor King, I too have a dream: America will not be judged by the promises that our politicians make, but by the deeds that create freedom in the world. We will not be judged by our pornographic films but by our citizens who travel abroad and are recognized as upstanding Americans. We will not be judged by our inconsiderate and judgmental media, but by a new media that is based only on truth. The world will look up to us again when we have implemented the policies that I have envisioned.

Maybe some of my dream has always been there. This was printed in a New Zealand Paper: February 5, 2006.

The Verdict on America: Not Guilty. Everyone talks about the weather, Mark Twain famously observed, but nobody does anything about it. Much like America's role in the world. Writing in Foreign Policy, Michael Mandelbaum says the gap between what the world says about American power (much of it hostile) and what it fails to do about it, is the single most striking feature of the 21st-century international relations. Historically, other great nations were always subject to a check on their power. Why not America? Mandelbaum explains: "First, the charges most frequently leveled at America are false. The United States does not endanger other countries, nor does it invariably act without regard to the interests and wishes of others. Second, far from menacing the rest of the world, the United States plays a uniquely positive global role. The governments of most other countries understand that, although they have powerful reasons not to say so explicitly." From humanitarian efforts, to peacekeeping and economic stability, the United States helps influence and balance the various equilibriums of the global power politics. Mandelbaum believes that any less of the role that America currently plays as the world's leader would make the world a far more dangerous and less prosperous place. "Never in human history has one country done so much for so many others, and received so little appreciation for its efforts," he writes.

First Saturday Of Each Month

Thank You for reading the book. Let's start electing the right people in 2010. See you at the rallies. I'll be the one with the sign that says: "Read my Book and Fix this Country"

E-mail me at howtosavetheusa@yahoo.com